Dear Reader,

A year ago, in February 2018, Harlequin Desire published *The Baby Claim*, the first book in my Alaskan Oil Barons series. Now here we are with the eighth—and last—book in the series, *The Secret Twin*. Wow, what a ride it's been! And I've enjoyed the opportunity to weave together this sweeping family saga.

How fitting that we started and completed the series in the month of Valentine's Day. What a fun time of year to celebrate the Steeles and Mikkelsons going from fierce business rivals to a close-knit family full of people each finding their happily-ever-after.

If you missed the first seven books in the series, they're all still available online. You can also find more info about each of them on my website: catherinemann.com.

Thank you for tuning in for the journey!

Cheers,

Catherine Mann

CATHERINE MANN

—

THE SECRET TWIN

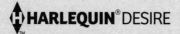

To Vickie Ostrander Gerlach, a dear friend and amazing beta reader! Thank you for cheering me on during the Alaskan Oil Barons journey.

ISBN-13: 978-1-335-60346-3

The Secret Twin

Copyright © 2019 by Catherine Mann

PLEASE RECYCLE
THIS PRODUCT IS RECYCLABLE

Recycling programs for this product may not exist in your area.

This edition published by arrangement with Harlequin Books S.A.

For questions and comments about the quality of this book, please contact us at CustomerService@Harlequin.com.

® and TM are trademarks of Harlequin Enterprises Limited or its corporate affiliates. Trademarks indicated with ® are registered in the United States Patent and Trademark Office, the Canadian Intellectual Property Office and in other countries.

Printed in U.S.A.

USA TODAY bestselling author **Catherine Mann** has won numerous awards for her novels, including both a prestigious RITA® Award and an RT Book Reviews Reviewers' Choice Award. After years of moving around the country bringing up four children, Catherine has settled in her home state of South Carolina, where she's active in animal rescue. For more information, visit her website, catherinemann.com.

Books by Catherine Mann

Harlequin Desire

Alaskan Oil Barons

The Baby Claim
The Double Deal
The Love Child
The Twin Birthright
The Second Chance
The Rancher's Seduction
The Billionaire Renegade
The Secret Twin

Visit her Author Profile page at Harlequin.com, or catherinemann.com, for more titles.

ALASKAN OIL BARONS - STEELE MIKKELSON FAMILY TREE

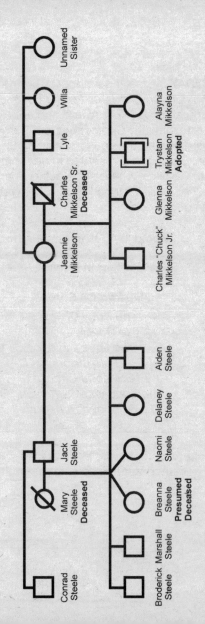

One

Breanna Steele didn't have much time to search the CEO's office at Alaska Oil Barons, Inc. If she got caught, the consequences could be catastrophic.

But she was out of options.

Brea needed answers and she didn't know who to trust. What if she chose wrong?

There were things far worse than prison.

She'd made a quick search of paperwork, and now she dropped into the sleekly modern leather chair behind the massive desk. She tried not to think about the times she'd visited this space as a child, when the office had been her father's. Saturday mornings coming here with her dad and her twin sister after breakfast at Kit's Kodiak Café. Playing hide-and-

seek under the huge desk, or watching cartoons on
the big screen at the other end of the office space,
sharing a blanket while they fell asleep on the leather
sofa.

Now the space belonged to another man, someone
outside of the family. The desk and the corner walls
of windows overlooking the frozen bay and distant
mountains were the same as she remembered. But the
rest of the space was now filled with new furniture—
sleeker, minimalist wood and leather pieces. Her father's office had been packed with family photos.
Ward Benally had only one picture on his desk. Him
with a little girl, elementary-school-aged, sledding.

She knew he wasn't married, but clearly this child
meant something to him. And that made him more
personable. More than just an arrogant leader of a
company that now belonged just as much to her rivals
as to her family. Her father's oil empire had merged
with the Mikkelsons' after his recent marriage.

Of course, Brea hadn't really been a part of any
of that, since they had believed she'd died as a young
teen.

Brea's conscience pinched. But her sense of sur-
vival dictated that she continue looking for the
damning information.

She pulled a flash drive from her purse and
plugged it into the computer. She'd lived off-the-
grid for years, and while some thought that meant
no computers, no communication with the outside
world, she'd actually learned to use the internet

without leaving a trail, building on knowledge she'd learned from her dad.

Learning to hack and code were skills stitched and threaded through much of her young life, before the airplane crash that had taken her from her family. She had shared that with her father. Once her mind was made up, Brea could accomplish anything. Dogged, unrelenting persistence. Also like Jack Steele. Her daddy.

Her chest went tight.

She blinked back tears and clicked through the keys, her fingers slick from the thin latex gloves she wore to keep her prints out of the office. Paranoid? Maybe. Maybe not. Bottom line, she couldn't be too careful.

Someone connected to this company had played a role in the airplane crash that had killed her mother. The crash that had changed Brea's life forever, in ways she still struggled to understand.

She had to have answers before she could put the past behind her, before she could feel safe here. Yes, she wanted to believe her relatives had nothing to do with such horrible treachery. Yet everything she'd learned pointed to someone in the Mikkelson family having been a part of the crash.

And now her father was married to the Mikkelson matriarch, merging their rival oil companies into Alaska Oil Barons, Inc. How surreal after their years of bitter competition and even outright enmity.

Almost too surreal. Like there might be a setup.

Hopefully she could find a clue here. If she didn't? Well, she didn't plan on giving up. She needed closure. But she also needed safety.

She wanted to reunite with her siblings, but she couldn't be sure where their loyalties lay. The risk of showing her hand was too high. She would be persistent. And patient.

Glancing at her watch, she checked the time. Earlier, she'd ferreted information out of the assistant that Ward would be in a conference call for most of the afternoon. But she didn't want to press that time to the limit.

A file name caught her attention, one simply titled with the date of the plane crash. She stifled a shiver at memories of the aircraft's plummet from the sky. The terror. Her mother's tight grip on her hand.

The air sucked from her lungs now. The same as it had then. A pull back to that day. The fear was a blood rush dragging her down. She could hear the whine of dying engines and the rustle of rapidly approaching earth.

Brea relived this moment more often than she cared to admit. Her body time traveling to the day that drew a line in the sand of her life. An eternal before and after.

A distraction Brea couldn't afford right now.

She clicked to copy the file to her flash drive, the urge to read it now overwhelming. Her heart raced, her speeding pulse hammering in her ears.

"What are you doing in my office?"

Brea jolted upright, the masculine voice making her heart stop.

Not only had she been discovered in the act of spying. But she'd been caught by the man himself. Ward Bennally. The new CEO of Alaska Oil Barons, Inc. A sexy dark-haired man wearing an Armani suit, cowboy boots...

And a heavy scowl.

Ward Benally had expected the first months as CEO of Alaska Oil Barons, Inc., would be challenging. He welcomed that. He lived and breathed his job.

It was his whole life.

It was all he had left.

He'd just finished a brutal board meeting that had almost broken out into a fistfight over disagreements about modifications to the oil pipeline. He'd come to his office to get documents he hoped would satisfy both sides. He'd also looked forward to a few moments alone to quiet his frustration.

Instead he found his office invaded by the last person he would trust alone with sensitive company data.

Brea Steele, the long-lost daughter of Jack Steele. The same daughter who'd posed as an employee of Alaska Oil Barons, Inc., not that long ago, to gain access to heaven only knew what kind of encrypted information. She could not be trusted. That should be obvious to everyone. But Jack was so happy to have his presumed-dead daughter back, they all had to put up with her, even though, by all rights, she should be under prosecution.

Ward eyed her with suspicion as she kept her hands out of sight, her brown eyes guarded as she sat at *his* desk.

"Well?" he repeated. "What are you doing in my office?"

Slowly, she rose from the buttercream leather chair, her hands now tucked in the back pockets of her black jeans. Jeans that clung to her long legs like a second skin. "I was waiting for you."

Her voice was cool and composed. Her sleek ponytail swished as she made her way around the desk, the silky glide of dark hair drawing his gaze like a hypnotic pendulum.

She was a smoke-and-mirrors show.

And his body reacted to her every time, no matter how often his brain reminded him she was trouble. "Looks to me like you were snooping around."

"I'm nosy." She shrugged, watching him through long dark eyelashes. "What can I say?"

"You call it nosy?" He strode forward, risking coming close enough to catch a whiff of…mint. "I call it breaking and entering."

"Your assistant let me in," she said neatly.

That gave him pause. He made a mental note to check her story. Even if it was true, she still should have been seated on the sofa or one of the guest chairs. "Did my assistant give you permission to use my computer?"

Her shrug called attention to her gentle curves. He snapped his attention back to the facts he knew about her. The woman before him had lied. Pretended to be someone else. Her actions were downright criminal. Brea could not be trusted. No matter how drop-dead sexy she looked in a turtleneck sweater.

"I just chose the most comfortable place to wait." She picked up the silver picture frame from his desk, no doubt to distract him. "Who's the kid? Cute little girl."

"Put that back." His voice was low, brooking no argument. The way he should have spoken to her about sitting at his desk. When she didn't put the frame down, he took it from her hands.

Ward had lost everything when his ex-wife left him, taking his stepdaughter with her. Since he wasn't little Paisley's biological father, he'd lost all rights to her after the divorce from Melanie. He'd hoped his ex would be open to letting them visit—or at least talk—but that hadn't been the case. His former wife just wanted to move on with her new life with her new husband.

Ward had been, for all intents and purposes, Paisley's dad since he'd started dating Melanie, when her daughter was eight months old. He and Melanie had married a year later. The marriage had lasted for six more years…longer than it would have if there hadn't been a child involved.

Ward wasn't sure he ever would have given up, for Paisley's sake. But Melanie had cheated, filed for divorce and was married to a guy twenty-five years her senior, wealthy, retired and ready to shower her with his money and time.

The metal on the frame dug into Ward's palm.

"Sorry." Brea twisted her hands in front of her, nails short, chewed down. "It was right out there for display."

"Only if you were behind my desk, in my chair." He placed the frame facedown so the picture of his stepdaughter wouldn't distract him. He glanced back up to find Brea's face showing a rare moment of vulnerability.

Calculated or legit? Experience with women told him it was more likely the former.

Her elegant throat moved with a slow swallow. "So, I wanted to see what my father's office felt like, if it was the same as when I was a child, spinning in the CEO's chair."

He stuffed back images of his child doing the same.

And yes, he was surprised Brea had gone for the heartstrings. "That was well-played."

"What do you mean?"

"You are throwing out that childhood memory to try and garner sympathy…or distract me from where you were sitting."

He wasn't letting her get away with invading his space. Heads would roll over her getting in here. For now, though, he couldn't afford to let her escape until he had answers.

"Okay, I sat in my father's chair because once I thought I would have a right to be there, that I would lead the company." She nibbled her bottom lip, slick with gloss. "For a moment I wanted to pretend that life had played out the way I'd hoped."

Was that another ploy to tug at his emotions and distract him? He wasn't sure.

Regardless, his eyes were drawn to her mouth.

He tamped down a rush of attraction. "You were still in my chair. At my computer."

All vulnerability slid from her face. She crossed her arms over her chest defiantly. "Fine. You're right. I had no business parking myself there. What do you intend to do about it?"

"I could call security." Ward's mouth tightened into a thin line. He met her brown eyes with an unrelenting stare. The kind of stare he'd perfected in long games of poker, after his divorce. The poker table was where he'd regained command and control. Honed his skills for leadership. For impassive demands.

"You could. And when they find there's nothing on me and it's just your word against mine?" Her voice was rich and sultry. Those dark brows arched…playfully?

"If they find nothing on you." He watched her face for signs he'd struck a chord.

Was it his imagination or did her eyes widen with fear? As fast as the look was there, it left.

"And my father? What will he think?"

Jack Steele would do anything to keep her here—in town, at the company, in the family—and they both knew it. Still, Ward bluffed. He was good at it. His fast-track career attested to that. "He's on the board, but that doesn't mean he can fire me."

She ran her fingers along the edge of the desk, the movement slow and intentional as she looked up at him. Fire flashed in those eyes. "He'll be upset and his opinion still carries a lot of sway with the board and investors."

It was rare someone called his bluff. Instincts told him she was a worthy adversary.

Which made her all the more attractive.

Damn.

"You're right. So, why were you in here when you know it could make things tougher for the two of you to reconcile?"

"I guess that proves I wasn't doing anything wrong." She toyed with the end of her sleek ponytail.

He chuckled softly, not tricked at all by her little hair twirl. "Are you sure you're not a lawyer like your twin? Because you sure do have a way with words."

"Must be genetics." She flicked her hair back over her shoulder, drawing his attention to the curve of her breasts, outlined by the formfitting black sweater.

He cleared his throat and backed up a step, needing air that didn't carry a minty scent. "Enough flirting."

"Flirting?" She smiled slowly. "Were you hoping I was flirting with you?"

Yeah, actually, he was.

And that was dangerous.

But not as dangerous as having her wandering around unchecked, peeking into the everyday operations of Alaska Oil Barons, Inc. It was bad enough she'd gotten away with it once. That was when she was in disguise and no one had an emotional connection to her. Now that the Steele family was emotionally vulnerable over her return after being presumed dead, there was no telling what they would let her do.

He needed to come up with a plan to keep her in his sights, sooner rather than later.

Brea needed to get out of Ward's office sooner rather than later.

How could she have let herself get caught up in flirting with him? Every second she remained here increased the chances of him finding the flash drive in her purse. She'd barely had time to peel off the latex gloves and stuff them away. If he'd seen them, he would have realized she'd been up to something shady for sure.

Although, if her fingerprints had been found on the keyboard, in the file cabinets or in the desk, she would have been in even worse trouble.

"I need to go." Was that breathy voice hers? She cleared her throat and started toward the door.

Except, Ward's broad chest was in her way. She should have worn heels. But she'd been thinking about stealth and not whether she could meet Ward's eyes once she got caught. Vibrant blue eyes, the color of an Alaskan lake, lightly iced over and ready to thaw.

"Of course." He nodded, waving her through the door. "After you." When she hesitated, he said, "Really, after you."

Only then did she realize she'd been standing, rooted to the spot, looking into his gaze like a starstruck, sex-starved idiot.

She forced a vampish smile onto her face. "I promise, I'm not going to work my wiles on your assistant to get through the door."

"Again."

She blinked. "What?"

"Get through my door...*again*." His smile matched hers, making her realize he'd seen right through her.

Was he as affected by a simple grin as she was? Because if so, then they were both in trouble. Her body was tingling from head to toe. There'd been a combustible chemistry between them from the moment they'd met. And the timing couldn't be worse, given the mess with her family.

The mess she *still* had to settle.

She couldn't afford the distraction of this man. Too bad his job put him firmly in the way of her goal of finding closure for her past. She needed to know who was responsible for blowing apart her family. For ending her mother's life.

And until she knew whom she could trust, she had to maintain a laser focus. Keeping him off-balance would help. "Who was the child in the picture?"

She nodded toward the metal frame he'd placed facedown on the desk. The Ward Benally in that picture seemed so different from the one before her. Against the surreal backdrop of a snowcapped-mountain range, he and the young child—maybe a four-year-old—leaned forward in a wooden sled. Snow wicked off in a wave to the side of the sled. Ward's blue eyes, somehow visible, were soft. Filled with joy. His protective arm was around the child, who was dressed in a puffy pink jacket and snow pants. Laughter was present on her little face.

"That's my stepdaughter." His smile faded, his face somber.

Mission accomplished in knocking him off-balance. So why did she feel so bad? "But you're not married."

"Not any longer." Tight voice. Tight response.

Off-balance indeed. A moment of guilt passed through her. The glimmer of pain in his words stung.

That shouldn't have mattered to her, but given their undeniable chemistry, it did. "I'm sorry."

He nodded toward the door again, not budging from his position. He obviously wanted to ensure she walked out first. "I need to get to work. As soon as I escort you from the building, I can do that."

She really should make tracks and get out with whatever info she'd gained. She's was risking too much by staying here, drawn in by Ward Benally's allure.

Striding through the door, she tried to ignore the

sensation of his eyes on her. One breath at a time. She forced her heart rate to slow in time with her steps. She kept her gaze forward, off the window view of Alaska—icy water, snow and mountains. All so familiar. She wondered how the memories of this place had become dulled during her years away in the isolated little Canadian village, where her "adoptive" parents lived, a close-knit community that had become her world after the plane crash.

"Benally," a deep voice rumbled down the corridor.

Her father's voice.

Brea froze.

Ice crackled through her veins at this next surprise. Nothing she'd planned from this data-gathering mission had gone as expected. But this next hiccup truly rattled her to the core.

She should have thought of the possibility of seeing her father when she came here. Should have been prepared. She was working on talking with her family, trying not to close doors until she figured out whom she could trust. But she usually had more time to prepare herself.

Was that Ward's hand on her back?

Her brain scrambled with too much to process at once. Her vision cleared, and she saw the conference room was half full—her father, his new wife and a slew of Mikkelson and Steele relatives, along with investor Birch Montoya and environmental scientist Royce Miller, husband to Brea's twin sister, Naomi.

Brea stumbled. Air sucked from her lungs again.

Even though she'd come back to Alaska last fall—albeit in disguise—it was still like a sucker punch coming face-to-face with Naomi. Seeing all her siblings was tough. But Naomi? They'd shared more than similar looks. They'd shared a bond.

Or so she'd thought.

When Brea had come to this office before, she'd half expected Naomi to recognize her even while she posed as Milla Jones. She'd chosen the fake identity to infiltrate the company and find out what had happened all those years ago. But when her initial snooping had been uncovered, things had gotten complicated. She'd just wanted to know who she could trust, to get answers about the past and gain vengeance for her mother.

And yes, maybe she'd had the tiniest hope that she could have her family back.

But Naomi hadn't even recognized her. There hadn't been a single spark of recognition. Even knowing it was irrational to expect Naomi to know her—even in disguise, even after all this time—that total loss of connection had still hurt.

Her father stepped from the doorway, into the corridor, the others still hanging back in the conference room, behind the glass window. "Good afternoon, Brea," her lumbering father said in that voice that sounded like he'd gargled rocks over the years. "I didn't know you were here."

Somehow he managed to look exactly like she remembered him from before the plane crash. Broad-chested. His eyes the unflinching blue of the Atlantic Ocean. Hair still dark and thick, although flecked with gray these days. As he looked at her now, she saw hope cross his angular jaw as his mouth relaxed into a small, nearly imperceptible smile.

That sure seemed to be the comment of the day. "I came by to speak with Ward."

Her father's eyebrows met, creasing his forehead. "What about?"

Her heart hammered again as she looked at Ward with panic. Was he going to rat her out? She wouldn't blame him. And she hated how easily she'd just lied. And lied poorly, for that matter. Could her inability to think quickly have had something to do with the distracting touch of Ward's hand on her back?

Just as she opened her mouth to spin out a better version of her fib, a breathless woman rushed up the hallway, toward them, pushing a stroller. It took Brea a moment to place her as Isabeau Mikkelson, wife of Trystan, mother of little Everett, and a media consultant.

The frazzled redhead thrust a binder toward Jack. "Here are the printouts of the guest list for the engagement party for Delaney and Birch, so you and Jeannie can work with them on the seating chart." She rushed to add, "And I locked down the vintage roulette wheel for the casino theme."

Smoothing her shoulder-length hair, Isabeau

smiled gently. A calming soul. One of the people Brea instinctively felt to be genuine. Besides, Isabeau wasn't connected to the Mikkelsons by blood. And Brea had to admit, that lack of connection made Isabeau intriguing as a potential information source. There was that old saying that those on the margins could see the center best. And damn, did Brea need a better vantage point.

Jack nodded. "Seating chart. Casino theme. Got it."

His words blurred together as Brea studied her family through the hall window. They were scattered around the conference room, some speaking in pairs, others clustered behind Jack.

Brea's gaze skirted to her baby sister, Delaney, a slender woman with dark wavy hair, standing quietly. Dressed in a simple red sweater dress and knee-high cognac-colored boots, Delaney visibly brightened as she leaned forward to look at the paper Isabeau handed to Jack Steele.

Brea swallowed hard. Memories of playing dress up with her sisters, decades ago, scrolled through her mind. Days of making bridal veils from towels with her sisters. They'd dreamed of planning those real family events together.

Her life was such a jumble.

Brea remembered her family, her childhood. But in the years that had passed since the crash, it felt like those memories had become unreliable. Thanks to the lies and betrayal of her "adoptive" parents, she questioned what was real…and what she wanted to believe.

There was so little she knew for certain. Such as how her mother had a special seal hunting knife called an ulu that she'd used to cut their pizza. Her mother's impossibly strong and reassuring "I love you" as the plane had plummeted.

Everything else? Up for debate and analysis.

The caress of Ward's hand on the small of her back pulled Brea back to the present. She looked at him, startled, curious.

His smile gave her only a moment's warning before he announced, "I guess this is as good a time as any to let them know our little secret."

Panic sent her heart racing. Had he seen her take off the gloves after all? Maybe there were cameras in his office?

"Um, let's talk about this."

"You're such a tenderhearted woman." His hand slid up her spine in a body-melting stroke that ended with his arm around her shoulders. His expression showed a warmth she'd never seen from him before. "It's sweet of you to worry what your family will think. I know they've only just gotten you back, but I think they'll understand the need to share you."

"Share *me*?" She was struggling for air.

Talk about being knocked off-balance. Her efforts to pull one over on her family had been amateur compared to this move. And she was too damned speechless to come up with a rebuttal as he tucked her closer to his side.

"Yes. Share you. With your boyfriend." Ward's grin dug dimples in his wind-weathered face before he announced, "Brea and I are dating."

Two

Ward was a man of action and swift decisions.

And he saw that this was the perfect opportunity to keep Brea in his sights—as his "girlfriend." Now he just needed to get Brea away from her family ASAP to convince her that he was right before she denied they were dating and blew up the whole charade.

"I'll be right back, after I see Brea to her car so she's not late for her dental appointment." Ward filled the stunned silence so he could direct the conversation. "Go ahead and get started without me. I'll catch up."

With a quick nod, he hustled her toward the elevator, as fast as possible, before the stunned Steeles and Mikkelsons could start asking questions. As he walked quickly down the corridor, thank heaven, she stayed at his side, for whatever reason. Shock? Curiosity? Or... Who knew what went on inside that woman's mind.

The minute the elevator door closed them inside, Brea stomped her foot, leveling him with eyes as dark as fire-hot coals. "Have you lost your mind? What the hell was that all about back there?"

He tapped the stop button, halting the elevator midfloor. "That was about keeping you close to my side. The snooping has to stop. At least while you're pretending to be my girlfriend, I can watch you."

Her eyes widened in shock. "You can't be serious. You actually expect me to pretend to be your girlfriend so you can keep tabs on me? And you think people will believe that we've been secretly dating?" She shook her head quickly, restlessly turning away, then back to him again. "You have got to be kidding."

"I'm dead serious." That much was true. His job was everything to him. He would not be made a laughingstock by a snoop who should just talk to her family...unless she had some darker motive. In which case, she should be kept under close scrutiny. He would be the one to take on that task because he was in charge. And yes, because of attraction crackling between them like sparks showing from a blazing fire. "I'm single. There are events I need to attend with a plus-one. This also saves me time."

"That's an absurd excuse." Her voice went higher

with frustration. "Be real. What could you have to gain from this charade? If you're that worried about little ole me, why not just install some security cameras?"

"You're right. I could up the security system to watch every inch of any space we control on the off chance I catch you getting up to something." He paused, and then pointed out logically, "And then, if I were successful, your dad and your siblings would forever see me as the person who revealed their princess to be an evil queen. This way, I can be more proactive."

"Princess? Evil queen? You're weird." Sighing, she furrowed her brow. "How is that different from catching me at something while I'm your pretend girlfriend?"

"I'm not weird. Just logical. If I'm watching you, you won't have a chance to be in that position. Besides, you'll get to stick close to me. And since you seem to be there every time I turn around, I have reason to believe that must hold some kind of appeal for you, too." He tugged her ponytail, testing the silky texture between his fingers, imagining it spread out over the pillow next to him. "And yes, there's more in it for me than just a plus-one for events. As a bonus, I gain acceptance by the board of directors. Being with you makes me a de facto member of the family."

Her eyebrows shot up in horror. "We are *not* getting married just to lock down your new job in the company."

"Of course not. I'm not that Machiavellian." He smoothed her silky ponytail back along her shoulder, her pupils widening with awareness at his touch. "But by the time that would be an issue, you and I can break up."

"I'm not dating you for that long." Then she rushed to add, "I'm not dating you at all. Start the elevator."

Ah, she'd mentioned dating. He was making progress. And that filled him with a surge of success. And desire. "We would only go out for a month, until the vote at the next general board meeting for all the shareholders."

She hesitated, worrying her bottom lip. "Then we just…what? We break up?"

He pulled his eyes off her moist lips.

"That's how it works, yes. You can even dump me." He winked, taking heart in her light chuckle. "And by all means, make it public and humiliating, in front of your entire family and all my friends—"

"You have friends?" Her deadpan words didn't match the hint of amusement in her eyes.

"I do." He nodded, leaning in such a way that he blocked the elevator buttons. Before long, someone would start it again, but he intended to make the most of their time alone for now. "I have to pay them to be my friends. But they stay loyal as long as I deliver the roll of quarters each week." Which wasn't totally true. He didn't have many friends, not even paid ones. He wasn't the sort to hang out with bud-dies. He was too busy working until midnight.

She scrunched her nose. "You really are weird."

"Maybe." He was certainly a workaholic. Al-though, so was most of her family. It was one of the reasons he now held this CEO position. "But the offer for you to dump me in a billboard fashion stands."

"How generous of you. Maybe I'll get one of my siblings to fly a seaplane with a banner." She lifted her chin, jaw jutting with signature Steele confidence that no amount of years away could erase.

"Trust me, my ego can take it."

She studied him for a moment, her exotic eyes narrowing. "Then what's in it for me?"

"Aside from getting to dump me? Isn't that enter-tainment and payment enough?" He thumped him-self on the chest in faux shock.

She rolled her eyes. "While that is an enticing proposition, I'm going to need a little more before I sign on to this plan."

He straightened, ditching the humor and closing the deal. "You'll keep me from ratting you out about being in my office. And you'll get more access to your family with me as an excuse for you to be in and out of this office."

"I'm listening." She waved him on, leaning a slim shoulder against the mirrored elevator wall. "Con-tinue…"

Her sweater pulled snug across her breasts as she folded her arms. His gaze followed the curve of her hip, which was cocked to one side. She drew him in, no doubt.

"I can be a buffer between you and your family." Which would give him the chance to gauge her motivations. No way was he going to let her tank this company. He'd always been a driven individual at work. But even more so now. His career was all he had left, and he refused to allow any threat to his professional reputation. "If you're feeling stressed or uncomfortable, cue me and we can leave."

"Or I could just walk out if they upset me."

He liked the confidence in her voice. But he also knew the situation with her family was far more complicated than that. "You could. But having a buffer so you could make a speedy, nonconfrontational exit would be easier."

"How so?" She looked skeptical.

"We come up with a safe word. If you say it in casual conversation, that lets me know you want to leave. I'll find an out so you don't have to make awkward excuses on the spot."

"Safe word?" Her eyebrows shot upward.

"Bear with me," he said. "I had this uncle who was a preacher. His wife used to get stuck at long functions and meals. So she came up with a conversational gimmick that let her husband know she needed to leave. Immediately."

"What was their word?"

"Words. Anchors aweigh. Which is technically two words, but you get the gist." Stifling a grin, he imagined his aunt working the safe word into their conversation.

A smile twitched at her lips, mesmerizing him. "That's a strange phrase."

"It worked." He enjoyed seeing her lighter hearted. He didn't want a real relationship, not after his bitter divorce, but he couldn't deny he was enjoying the banter. And she was smoking hot, to boot.

A part of him was hoping she'd say yes to this for more than just reasons related to her family. He couldn't deny he was drawn to her. And since he was going to be leading this company, he needed to work through the attraction to her sooner rather than later. Issues left unaddressed became distractions.

And she was already a major distraction.

"Okay then. What do you suggest?"

He thought for a moment, his eyes landing on a framed painting of a home with stone figureheads worked into the architecture. "Gargoyle."

"Gargoyle?" She burst out laughing.

Tension faded from her expression to be replaced by a smile that knocked the air from his lungs. Damn, she was a beautiful woman. Pulling his attention off her delicate features and back on the task at hand, he took heart in making progress with her.

He'd been in business long enough to know when he'd closed the deal. "Do we have an agreement?"

Her eyes narrowed, but her smile didn't fade. "Just until the next general board meeting."

"One month," he said, confident now that he

could win her over to extending their time together if needed. For now he'd made major progress. He was going to be able to watch over her. And if she was up to something, he would find out what.

And he had to admit, spending time with her wouldn't be a hardship in the least. She drew him with everything from her sexy curves to the sweep of her eyelashes when she cast a glance his way... She was definitely a distraction he needed to work out of his system.

"So, this is just pretend?"

"As long as you say so. And if you're ever uncomfortable, just remember." He winked, tapping the start button on the elevator. "Gargoyle."

Even five hours later, in her new one-bedroom apartment, Breanna's brain was still reeling from Ward's surprise proposition. Sure, he was smart, sexy, and powerful, and while all of that drew her in, she'd been holding strong.

Until she'd been knocked off-balance by his surprise sense of humor.

She should have put up more of a fight. Or extracted additional tradeoffs. But she'd been unsettled by being caught in his office, and then unexpectedly seeing her family, all of which had lowered her defenses.

Checking her emails on her phone now, she leaned against the cool counter space. The granite pressed into her skin as she skimmed her inbox to see if any of her clients needed anything. As a virtual shopper for those who were homebound or in need of help, her hours were a little inconsistent. No new emails since she'd checked an hour ago, which meant she could turn her attention back to the blueberry and raspberry muffins she was baking, needing to do something productive since she hadn't managed to find anything useful on the flash drive yet.

Frustration filled her. She forced herself to focus on the routine of baking. Grounding herself in the moment. Muted light filtered in through the windows, dappling the dark wood floors and small kitchen area.

She was so grateful to have found this space for her time here in Alaska while she sifted through the rubble of her past. Her uncle's new wife—Felicity Hunt Steele—had offered this space to sublet. Other Steele relatives had suggested Brea stay with them, but the stress of that was more than Brea could wrap her head around.

A chirp of the kitchen timer in the shape of a plump, plucky hen snapped Brea to attention. She grabbed the gold polka-dot oven mitt from the kitchen counter and peeked into the oven. A wave of warmed-berry scent rode the air, escaping through the open oven door. Such a sweet scent. It made her stomach growl in anticipation. A memory flashed through her mind of berry picking with her siblings and parents, of her dad telling her to avoid the white berries, which were poisonous.

She swallowed hard before the past could swamp her with too many recollections at once. The faster they came, the tougher it was to gauge which ones were real.

A dish towel in hand, she pulled the muffins from the pan, one by one. Since she'd shed her disguise as Milla Jones and returned to Alaska last month, she'd been spending controlled amounts of time with her family. Always with others present, including her uncle's new wife, who was a social worker.

Felicity had even given Brea a list of therapists. Not necessarily to facilitate a reunion. But to make sure she kept a clear head and didn't get hurt. Brea had called numbers on that list until she found a counselor she was comfortable with, one who could help her.

She wasn't sure if she would reconcile with her family or not, but she needed some semblance of peace with her past before she could move on with the future. She'd known that on some level when she'd come to Alaska, posing as Milla Jones.

And how did her attraction to Ward play into that? It was a dangerous distraction. She would have to keep a close guard on her hormones around this man.

A rapid knock caused her door to shudder, startling her. Rattling awake other memories she did her best to keep locked up in the corners of her mind.

Her gut clenched with tension. She'd spent so many years in that minimalist, off-the-grid community, she still wasn't used to having such a cluttered world. She walked from her kitchen, through the living area to the front door. She peered through the keyhole…and sighed with relief.

Felicity stood with Tally Benson, Felicity's friend and the woman who was dating Marshall Steele. These two were easy company, since they weren't a part of her past. Brea clicked through all three locks and opened the door.

"Hello," Felicity said, holding up a basket full of pampering bath items—salts, a loofa and towels. She had a way of taking care of everyone, perhaps something to do with her chosen career as a social worker. "We've brought housewarming gifts."

Tally carried a wicker laundry hamper. "All natural cleaning supplies, just for you."

While trust was difficult, these two women were the only ones Brea had met since her return whom she felt at least partially comfortable with. Although, her relationship with Tally was still complicated. Tally's father had been the mechanic who worked on the airplane before the crash. He'd committed suicide because of his guilt over what had happened. No one yet knew the full extent of the details of the crash, and Tally's father had taken his secrets to the grave. But at least the man's name offered a place to start searching for answers.

"Thank you so much," Brea said, touched by their kindness, and a little overwhelmed too, especially with the berry-picking memory still so fresh in her mind. "Um, please come inside."

Felicity hesitated. "Are you sure we're not imposing?"

Brea laughed softly. "Of course I'm sure, not that I would turn you away. It is your condo and you've been kind enough to sublease it to me for next to nothing."

"You've done me a favor," Felicity said without hesitation. "Now I'm able to live with Conrad without this place hanging over my head unused."

Brea gestured for the duo to come into the apartment, appreciating the down-to-earth nature of both of these women. "The gifts are lovely. You two didn't have to do this."

"Conrad sends his thanks as well for the help with my lease," Felicity called over her shoulder as if they all didn't already know Conrad Steele could have paid the rent for her apartment multiple times over. Felicity continued to work at the local hospital, where she'd been today, and her hair was still swept back in a French twist. "You can soak out the tension."

Tally strode past, her red ponytail swishing. Felicity had taken her under her wing not too long ago. Tally had been a housekeeper and now attended college on a scholarship to become a social worker, as well. "If you need any help, just call me."

Felicity set the basket on the coffee table, cellophane wrapping crinkling. "Although, for the record," she said with a smile and an elegantly arched eyebrow, "I did leave the place spotless."

"You did," Brea agreed, chewing her bottom lip.

It seemed so surreal to have the two women move so effortlessly into her life. Making friends was hard for her after all she'd been through. Even though the small Canadian community had been welcoming, her adoptive parents had been guarded with others. She'd been alone, not even sure she could trust her own instincts, for a long time. Being told that her biological family was deeply corrupt. She was safer away from them. "Thank you for coming over. Both of you. Could I offer you something to drink?"

"Well, actually—" Tally paused, unloading the cleaning supplies and stowing them under the kitchen sink "—we did have another reason for coming by."

Brea's stomach knotted with nerves. Closing the front door was tough, especially when she wanted to run. "What would that be?"

Felicity pinned her with a knowing gaze. "When did you start dating Ward Benally?"

Brea exhaled with relief that they weren't going to grill her about her past. Only to have her nerves return with a vengeance over the mention of her fake boyfriend.

Her very sexy, surprisingly charming fake boyfriend.

She really wasn't ready for fielding questions about Ward.

"The relationship started very recently." Very. Very. Recently.

"Well, I'm not surprised at all." Tally pulled out a barstool from behind the counter and sat, her boot heels resting on the lowest rung. "I noticed the chemistry between the two of you at the fund-raiser last month."

Had it been obvious even then? Brea had felt the sparks, but she'd liked to think she'd hidden her reaction. Apparently not.

Felicity leaned over to look at the baked goods. "Was that when it started, at the fund-raiser?"

Brea *hmmed*, taking a bite to fill her mouth and avoid talking. Too bad no one was around who could help if she shouted *gargoyle*. "Anyone want a muffin?"

Tally pulled napkins from a counter holder. "Yes, please. Although I do hear you trying to change the subject. I imagine you're wondering how much you can trust the two of us."

True, but not the sort of thing Brea expected to hear voiced aloud.

"Although—" Felicity broke a muffin in half, then pinched off a bite "—that's an unwinnable proposition, since no matter what we say, there's really no way to prove you can trust us at this point. Trust takes time."

How long? Brea wished she knew. "Spoken like a counselor."

"Because I am one." Felicity swept up a crumb into her hand and then into the sink. "For what it's worth, Tally and I are both new to the Steele family realm. As such, we weren't a part of the old days, the old problems and whatever happened then. But we're here for you now and want to be your friends, as well as family."

Brea wanted to believe that. "I'm still getting to know everyone again."

"Give it time." Felicity squeezed her hand.

Tally scrunched her freckled nose, grinning. "And while you're giving it time, tell us… Does Ward kiss as incredibly as it seems he would?"

Brea felt the heat steal up to her face. That particular topic was occupying far more of her thoughts than it should. Her cell phone dinged with an incoming text and Brea embraced the excuse to step away from the intense conversation. She wanted—needed—a chance to regain her footing. "Excuse me for a moment. I need to check that."

She raced to scoop her phone off the coffee table and turned her back on the two women, who seemed content to snack on their muffins. She thumbed the text open to find…

A message from Ward.

Butterflies launched inside her. She shouldn't feel this excited, but she did. And she couldn't afford to be distracted by hormones, not when she finally had a real chance at the answers she craved.

Then she read his message, and it was as if the floor fell away beneath her feet.

I'll be by at seven to pick you up for supper with the Steeles. Be ready to help me make nice with all your family members on the board.

So much for keeping a lock on her emotions. Her body was already on fire at just the thought of seeing him again.

Ward knew he was pushing it with the impromptu dinner out with the Steeles. But he'd wanted to see Brea, and this was the fastest, easiest way to lock that down. He didn't want to think overlong about how damn much he looked forward to seeing her. Better to keep it simple. This was a short-term thing between them. He was married to his work.

So he could just enjoy the moment, and yes, this potential for a fling. By the time she figured out he had set up the get-together, it would be too late. She would already be sitting at the table.

Would she be mad?

Almost certainly.

Was she sexy when riled up?

Absolutely.

He'd been surprised by how much he wanted to see her again. How his intentions had shifted so quickly from wanting to keep an eye on her to wanting to follow through on their attraction. Now he saw that his dating idea had no doubt sprung from the heat that flared whenever they were near each other. But if that played out into a fling, he could handle it. His emotions were locked down tight after the number his ex had pulled on him.

He guided his SUV through the night, headlights striping bands of illumination into the snowy air ahead, Brea in the passenger seat, quiet since he'd picked her up. Likely there were other ways to keep watch over her, but this was far more…entertaining.

Snowflakes sprinkled down, glinting in the beams. Brea looked stunning sitting beside him in a royal-blue wool coat and black leather boots. Her hair was draped over one shoulder in an appealing onyx water-fall. She sat so still and regal, he would have thought her unaffected by this evening together if not for the way she picked at her short fingernails.

Low music played from the speakers, his playlist of classical guitar music.

Brea sighed heavily.

He stifled a grin. "You seem angry, my dear."

"My dear?" She turned in her seat toward him, the dash lights casting her face in seductive shadows. "Are you serious? No one's watching us."

"But you are my dear, new girlfriend." Flicking his eyes from the road, he met her eyes.

"*Fake* girlfriend. And since no one's around, let's make some ground rules."

"Such as?" He gripped the leather steering wheel as he accelerated. The sound of the exhaust mingled with the few other trucks on the road.

"You could start telling me about these plans of yours—the whole dating thing and going to the family dinner—earlier than a few minutes ahead of time."

He didn't bother noting that he'd given her a few hours to prepare. He got her point. "If I had given you too much advance notice, would you have come along?"

"You'll never know, will you? You didn't give me the chance to decide." She crossed her arms, head turning away from him to look out the window at the snow lightly falling from the sky.

"I do know," he retorted without hesitation. Then felt the need to own up to planning this. His gut served him well in business. He would think of this arrangement with her like business. "If I'd made the reservations for later in the week, you would have come up with excuses."

"That's my right."

"Yes, it is." SUV idling at a stoplight, he waited, knowing she would come to the obvious conclusion.

"All right, but if I decline, then I don't get the inside scoop on my family. Fine." She huffed in exasperation. "So how about from now on, you give me the opportunity to say yes or no and see what happens."

"Fair enough. I will take that under consideration."

Mouth twitching into a satisfied smile, he approached the one-story brown cottage, which had been turned into a restaurant, more eager for her approval than he wanted to admit.

The historic brown building with cream trim seemed bright against the gray backdrop of February skies. Guiding the SUV into the parking lot, he readied himself for this next encounter.

A favorite place of his. Simple from the outside, like a small home, but the restaurant boasted top-notch Alaskan seafood cuisine, the menu changing weekly. With only a dozen tables, it offered an intimate setting. He'd booked the place for the entire night to avoid prying eyes as they became comfortable with other.

He passed the keys to the valet and joined Brea under the covered walk leading to the front door. He clasped her elbow to make sure she didn't slip, even though the path had been shoveled and salted. The simple touch launched a wave of heat through him. Her quiet gasp told him she wasn't immune either. The pace of her breathing increased, puffing tiny clouds of air into the night.

He paused outside the door, turning to face her, her eyes locking with his. He lifted a curl of her hair and stroked the length of it, testing the silky texture between his fingers. Her eyes went wide with awareness. He understood the draw well.

More than this ruse, than her family, it was that draw that had brought them both here tonight.

The door swung wide, a host greeting them with a smile as the warmth gusted out. "Welcome to Chez Louis, Mr. Benally. Most of your party has arrived. They're enjoying drinks in the lounge. Ma'am, if I could take your coat?"

The small crowd of Steeles and Mikkelsons already filled the dining area, most of them standing beneath vintage antler chandeliers. Conversation wafted over in murmurs.

No sooner had Ward and Brea passed off their coats than his date bolted away, under the guise of talking to Felicity and Delaney. The duo stood by a crackling fire, sipping wine. Waitstaff walked from person to person, offering roasted-eggplant pâté on pita bread and gnocchi with cambozola and red crab. Another waiter flourished a tray with Alaskan oysters and Neapolitan seafood mousse.

But Ward's attention was still on Brea. His smile faded. He didn't want to frighten her. When he'd roped her into this pretend relationship, he'd been so focused on protecting the company, he hadn't thought much about what she'd been through, losing her family, for all intents and purposes kidnapped. He needed to weigh his next move carefully to protect the business. And yes, to protect this woman too, if she was somehow as vulnerable as she'd looked in that flash before she'd retreated.

A tap on the shoulder had him looking away to turn and find Broderick Steele, Brea's oldest brother. "We need to have a talk. Are you actually dating my sister?"

"Why is that a question? I already announced that we are, and we came here together." Had Brea said something to tip off her brother? Ward studied the man in front of him—the eldest Steele was a carbon copy of his father.

"You barely know her," Broderick said. "She's

hardly speaking to our family. We don't know if we can trust her. Shall I keep listing the reasons why this seems like the strangest relationship ever?"

Broderick was sharp from years in the boardroom. But so was Ward.

"She's an attractive woman." His gaze landed on her all over again, enjoying the way she looked in her red sheath dress with long sleeves and a low back. "Circumstances drew us together. We have chemistry. It's nothing serious at this point, but we're giving it a go. How's that for a list?"

"She's fragile." Broderick's shoulders braced protectively as he tightened his grip on his lowball glass.

"You clearly don't know Brea—the woman she is now—as well as you think." Even considering that moment of fear in her face, he knew how brave she must be to face all of them after what she'd been through.

But brave didn't necessarily equate with honest.

"That could be true," Broderick conceded, tipping his drink from one side to the other, making the ice cubes clink against cut crystal. "I'm not sure anyone does know who she is now, since she's playing things so close to the vest. What if your relationship explodes in your face?"

Ward glanced across the room to where Brea stood with the other women by the thick cream-colored curtains. Her dark features schooled into practiced neutrality. "Then that would be a damn shame, but I don't see what it has to do with my contract with the company."

Broderick's eyebrows raised as his face became tight, foreboding as a winter storm. "It could make things awkward for you with the family if you two are tangled up with each other."

"Could. But it won't. I'm a professional." And if Brea really was intent on harming the company in some way, he was the only one likely to push hard enough to figure it out. Her family seemed to just want her back, no matter what she'd done.

He understood that feeling well after losing his stepdaughter. But he couldn't let it jeopardize what he was building here at Alaska Oil Barons, Inc. He had big plans for the company, working with Royce Miller to implement his inventions for the safer transportation of fuel and alternative energy sources. Delaney Steele was also an advocate with strong connections. He had a chance to make a difference.

Broderick eyed him skeptically. "Do you actually think life is that simple?"

"Sometimes it is. Sometimes it isn't," he answered as honestly as possible, given the circumstance.

"Okay then, I'll make this clear and simple for you." Broderick's voice dropped an octave as he leaned closer. "Be careful with my sister. Because even if I don't know exactly who she has become, she is—and always will be—my sister. If you hurt her, there won't be a place in Alaska remote enough for you to hide."

"Message heard." Ward met Broderick's icy gaze with all the warmth of a tropical island. With a board-room smile, he inclined his head. "Now I have a date. With your sister."

And despite all the warnings—from Broderick, and from his own wary nature—Ward very much looked forward to kissing her good-night on her doorstep.

Three

If someone had told her a year ago that she would have a subdued casual dinner out with her family, Brea would have called them crazy. But with Ward at her side, she'd faced the Steeles—and the questionable Mikkelsons—through a whole five-course meal.

She'd almost managed to quell her nerves. Almost.

And now that she stood outside her apartment door with the sexy new CEO of Alaska Oil Barons, Inc., her heart raced. He stared down at her with mesmerizingly blue eyes, seeming to see deep inside her. Was that an illusion? Or did Ward Benally somehow have insights into her that her own family—and even she herself—lacked?

The idea was crazy, of course. He was only going

through with this dating scheme to keep tabs on her. But she couldn't deny that their connection felt personal. And that, despite all the reasons she shouldn't trust him, she felt a level of ease in his presence.

Except for right now, when she also felt something dangerously close to…temptation.

"Dinner was nice. The food was delicious." She needed to bring the evening to a sensible close. Thank him and be done with it. "You were a gentleman. I appreciate that you respected my boundaries."

The location had been public enough to avoid confrontations, while also staying away from prying eyes. She was touched by his thoughtfulness, his intuitive understanding of what would be easiest for her. Touched, and surprised.

"You didn't use the safe word even once," he teased, his hand resting on the doorframe beside her, his shoulders broad and the stubble along his jaw an alluring shadow.

She swallowed to clear her suddenly dry mouth. "Because I couldn't remember what it was."

A lie, of course. To cover the fact that she'd actually felt sort of safe with him all evening long.

"Gargoyle." He winked, his blue eyes glimmering with mischief.

"Got it. I won't forget again."

Was there a safe word to protect her against the draw of this man?

Fiddling with the fringes of his wool scarf, Ward seemed to take his time before speaking. "Your family's trying hard to respect your space while welcoming you back into the fold."

She wanted that to be true. But trust was difficult to come by after all she'd been told by the couple who'd rescued her. Her recovery after the crash had been lengthy, and at the start they hadn't known who she was. Then they'd told her that her family had given up looking for her. Now she knew they'd kept her secluded, kidnapped and brainwashed. Her counselor said she suffered from Stockholm syndrome. And because they'd lied, that had crumbled her confidence when it came to believing other people, too. Not that she intended to share all of that with this man, who had questionable motives of his own.

So she stayed silent. Waiting. Wondering why she didn't just say good-night and slide into her apartment. Alone.

Ward's gaze held hers. "There are a lot of you Steeles."

She wished she could see into his thoughts as easily as he seemed to divine hers. "And your point is?"

"Just that they seem to care. They seem to think of you as one of their own." He shrugged his broad shoulders as he took a step toward her.

The distance between them was electric.

"Gargoyle." She swallowed, but didn't back away.

He stilled, head tipped to the side. "You want to leave?"

"Leave this conversation." And still she didn't go into her apartment.

"Okay then… The casino party is still a couple of days away. I think we should make arrangements for another date." He eased back a step, giving her space. "Just to be sure people don't question our devotion to each other. What would you suggest we do next?"

Now, that sounded like a loaded question. "You're in charge of the dates."

"I'm a modern guy, completely okay with you choosing what we do between now and your sister's engagement party."

She mulled over ideas, but she wasn't one for hobbies. Her adoptive family had been hardworking, their community insular and self-sustaining. She'd felt safe there, accepted, loved. Her adoptive parents had convinced her the outside world was dangerous—and she saw now that their fears were overblown. But in many ways, they had treated her well, like the child they'd always wanted and never had. In spite of their betrayal, she couldn't bring herself to hate them.

Damn, but her life was all so confusing.

Her mind wandered back to the time before the crash. Her mind filled with memories of ice fishing with her dad. Of horseback riding with her twin sister. Of climbing into the tree house with her brother Marshall to read—he always preferred quiet, his thick head of curls falling forward over his forehead.

All those memories, though, still felt too questionable, given how much she was working to piece everything together. She should devote time to digging through more data in the files she'd copied from Ward's computer.

Should.

But she wasn't.

There was also something compelling about spending time with her family, especially with Ward as a buffer. He led conversations, allowed her to be quiet when she wanted to observe and process.

The fake dating arrangement could actually benefit her more than she'd ever guessed.

Either that or she was justifying wanting to indulge this attraction just a little while longer.

"Let's get coffee and shop for books," she found herself saying. "Pick me up tomorrow, after seven."

"It's a date," he said, dipping his head to cover her mouth with his.

Surprise stilled her for a moment. The warmth and pressure of his lips on hers was a sudden, pleasant jolt to her senses, drawing all her focus to that place where they touched. The scent of his aftershave tantalized her as he gently deepened the kiss. His tongue touched hers, stroked, and she found herself swaying closer. Her body was ahead of her brain.

Before she could question herself further, though, sensation took over, nerve endings tingling to life, pleasure flowing through her veins. She swayed forward, her breasts lightly skimming against the hard wall of his chest. Her hands slid up to his shoulders. His low growl of approval rumbled between them, and he brought her closer. His tongue carried a lingering taste of dessert and a hint of something else. A breath mint maybe?

Her senses were awash in desire.

Her breath caught. Her fingers fisted against his jacket, gripping him tightly.

The heat and strength of him was apparent even through the wool, and it stunned her to realize how much she wanted to lean in closer. To part the fabric and feel more of him, test and learn the texture of his skin.

He angled back to look into her eyes, and she knew he was giving her control, letting her make the next move. Or not.

Breathing hard, she couldn't deny that she wanted him. She was all the more tempted by his restraint, a quality she appreciated. Admired.

Still, things were moving too fast. Her world was in turmoil.

And this wouldn't be her only chance to be with him.

Before she could succumb to the temptation to invite him inside, she spun away and slipped into her apartment, barely hanging on to the tattered shreds of her control.

She didn't want the night to end, but she would wait.

She *had* to wait. Be certain she wasn't making a mistake.

Because even as she tipped her head back against

the door inside her apartment, she was already anticipating their next date.

Shopping for books had never sounded so appealing, when she'd be in the company of the sexiest man she'd ever met.

Ward had wined and dined women. A five-star dinner was a surefire way to get himself out of the doghouse when he'd been married to his ex.

So he'd been caught unaware by Brea's request last night for a simple coffee date, along with book shopping at a local two-story establishment. Although *shopping* wasn't quite the right word for his date's approach to the shelves. Her walk down each aisle was something more akin to worship. She read the spine of each title, touching some reverently.

She gave an elegance to skinny jeans that drew him like a magnet. Turning a corner, she headed for the used-book section, toward the ladder. She climbed up two rungs, her soft red-and-black plaid shirt hugging her curves. Loose hair swaying, she leaned toward the shelf, smiling. The curve of her lips sent his thoughts chasing back to last night. To that spark between them that had leapt into something so very intense during that kiss.

It had been all he could do to walk away from her door last night.

For a moment he could have sworn she had considered taking things to the next level by inviting him into her bed. Maybe the next time they kissed, she wouldn't want to stop.

He certainly hoped that was the case, because thoughts of her were turning him inside out. Considering a fling was one thing. Having her occupy his thoughts so fully was another matter altogether. Obsession was not an option.

She climbed down from the ladder and picked up another book, her fingers stroking over the leather binding. Brea appeared lost in her own world as her hair waterfalled down her back. She was a siren indeed, her curves and the silken glisten of her hair calling to him.

Her beauty almost helped him push back the painful memory of another bookstore outing. Two years ago, he'd taken his stepdaughter to lunch and then out to buy a stack of books for her summer reading.

His mind filled with heartbreaking images of her smile when she found the new superhero-canine story she'd been looking for, her excitement when the store clerk had given her a bookmark with a picture of the fictional dog on it. Ward had promised they would read the first chapter together later that week, but it was a moment that had never happened because Melanie had left him, taking Paisley with her. Losing his little girl had torn his heart out, and he didn't intend to put himself in that vulnerable position ever again.

Clearing away the lump in his throat, he stopped

beside Brea, who was thumbing through a mythology collection. "Would you like a refill on the coffee?"

She turned to him with startled eyes, then blinked back to a more neutral expression. "Yes, please. Extra milk. Extra sweetener."

"As ordered." He pulled his hand from behind his back, already holding what she'd ordered. He'd listened. He tuned in to everything she said.

Not just because he needed to search out any possible hidden agenda.

And to be honest with himself, even if she did have an agenda, he still wanted to sleep with her.

"You know what I like?"

He let the double entendre pass. For now. "I paid attention to your order."

"That, too. Thank you." Cradling the cup in her hands, she eyed him over the top. "What would you have done if I'd said no just now?"

"Then I guess the coffee would have gone into the garbage." He pulled his other hand from behind his back. "Along with mine." He took a swallow of his steaming java while the store music swapped to a light jazz tune.

Foot traffic around the shelves was quiet in this section, although a student with bright red hair and a leather backpack passed now and then, singing to whatever played through the earbuds.

Brea stood in a beam from the track lighting

streaming down. After her sip of coffee, she sighed with bliss. "You don't have to romance me."

The hardwood floor squeaked as she shifted her feet.

"I'm attracted to you, and I consider myself a man of finesse." It didn't appear as if she wanted a long-term attachment, which made them a good match for an affair.

If only he could trust her, this would be an easy call, since he wanted her as much as air.

Although, the fact that he couldn't trust her would also protect him emotionally if they did indulge in a fling.

"I noticed." Her nose scrunched with her smile.

"Good. And the more we know about each other, the more authentic our dating ruse will seem to your family." He pulled the book from under her arm and set it on a table by a two-seat sofa tucked in the corner of the store. He motioned for her to sit.

Then he joined her, his thigh against hers, the intimacy of the quiet space wrapping around him. The floral scent of her shampoo teasing his every breath.

She set her coffee down, her brown eyes troubled. "You must realize I'm using you as a buffer with them. Those were the terms for our pretend relationship."

"Of course. And I don't have a problem at all with you using me as much as you like." Taking a sip, he appreciated the bitterness of his black coffee. The way even the scent of the beans kept him alert.

She laughed softly. "You are a strange man."

"A strange man who's piqued your interest." He could see it in her eyes. Feel the crackle in the air between them.

"How is it you manage to make a trip to the corner bookstore seem risqué?"

"You bring it out in me." His eyes lingered on her lips for a moment before he met her gaze, finding a heat that met and matched his own.

He dipped his head, angling his mouth along hers. Not for long. While it was private in this aisle for the moment, he couldn't count on that for long. The hum of voices around the store was muted through his passion-fogged senses, but he maintained enough cognizance to know he and Brea were too close to being discovered. And he wouldn't disrespect her with public displays. He grazed a quick, final kiss along her lips.

As he drew back, he found her eyes warm and dazed with desire. He understood the feeling well. Being this near her turned him inside out. So much so, he ached to get her alone, which was contrary to the whole fake-couple idea. But a quick trip… Hmm…that was simple to pull off with the corporate jet at his disposal. He wouldn't even have to be disconnected from work during a twenty-four-hour date.

"May I have my coffee?" she said, her voice husky.

"Of course." He passed it over, her fingers brushing his, his plan coming into crisp focus. "If you find a couple of books to read, it would help you pass the time on the plane."

"On the plane?" She paled.

"To get coffee—the best. You choose. Guatemala? Tanzania? Kenya? Hawaii? Say the word and you can wake up in the morning to java bliss."

He gestured toward the world map on the wall, a vintage print from the early twentieth century. The chart matched the rest of the travel motif of the bookstore. Old cameras, sextants and suitcases populated the store. A cozy atmosphere with this incredibly sexy woman.

"Taking me to another country for coffee is undoubtedly a romantic gesture, but I'm good with this." Her hands trembled, and she set the coffee down again before twisting her fingers together on her lap.

But he didn't miss the signs of her nerves. For a moment he thought it had to do with him, but then he thought back and realized she had first looked upset when he'd mentioned the plane.

Damn.

He should have remembered the crash she'd experienced. She seemed so fearless, though. He'd lost sight of what she'd been through, a trauma that would leave anyone with a boatload of apprehension.

"The offer stands," he said gently. "But we can adjust the plans. I'm open to whatever you want."

"I'll be fine with this." She picked up her cup again and took a long swallow.

"You're a cheap date."

"You haven't seen how many books I plan to buy." Smiling, she stood and walked back to the racks, her fingers grazing the book spines. "What do you like to read?"

His mind filled with the children's books he'd read to his stepdaughter. They'd had a set routine. Thirty minutes an evening of reading. Even when he was away on business, he made arrangements to Skype their story time. She often asked for more, and right now he would give anything to give her those extra minutes she'd requested.

"Business reading. Topics like financial research, corporate leadership—things like that," he answered gruffly, pushing aside thoughts of his stepdaughter asking for one more chapter. "What about you, Brea?"

Her eyes sparkled. Turned wistful as she patted the stack in her lap. "Anything. Everything."

He tapped the novels in her hands. "Do you not read digitally?"

"Now I do. At my other home, I read faster than they could restock books." She looked down at the growing stack of books in her arms, her gaze pensive. "This is a treat."

His conscience pinched. Part of this ruse meant placing her in her family's path more frequently than before. What if she wasn't guilty of anything more than curiosity? "Are you sure you're okay going to the casino party?"

"I went out to dinner with them. I think I can handle a big party, where there are plenty of distractions to keep me from speaking to people I wish to avoid."

He wondered if she meant anyone in particular. He hadn't noticed nuances like that last night at dinner, but he would try to be more cognizant of subtleties like that going forward. Especially if he was going to keep an eye on what she was up to. He had to stay alert and not be distracted by the attraction. If they pursued it, he could only indulge if he kept his focus where it belonged. On his new job at Alaska Oil Barons, Inc.

"But there will also be a lot of curious eyes on you."

And if she did have an alternative agenda, a party like that might reveal any and all accomplices. He didn't want to think like that. But he needed to remain vigilant. Aware.

"So, you planned the dinner yesterday to be just the family out of concern for my feelings?"

"Of course not." He nudged her knee with his. "That kind of sensitivity would do serious damage to my reputation as a boardroom shark."

"Well, we can't have that now, can we? It wouldn't be good for the company."

"Spoken like a true Steele." Something he would do well to remember.

They were a ruthless lot when it came to business.

Like him. Which meant he was better off not feeling sorry for her. He needed to keep his sights firmly set on keeping the corporation safe.

And if he and Brea shared a bed along the way?

All the better.

Brea walked into her sister's engagement party with her head held high, her grip on Ward's arm tight. It was a double-edged decision to touch him this way. Yes, she needed bracing to face this event. But the handsome man beside her filled out his tuxedo so perfectly that she found herself thinking about the kisses they'd shared, and ended up feeling unsteady on her feet.

"Are you okay?" he asked, his blue eyes full of deep concern.

Pull it together, she told herself. The last thing she wanted was for him to know how deeply he affected her.

"I'm fine. I will be an attentive, adoring date." She rubbed a thumb and index finger together, attempting to quell her nerves.

He'd opted for them to arrive after the sit-down dinner and to make their appearance during dessert and dancing so she wouldn't have to make chitchat. Another thoughtful move from a man who worked so very hard to appear heartless. She'd told him that seeing her family at a crowded event would be easier. And she'd genuinely believed that to be the case when she'd said it.

She was wrong.

Her world had been so sparsely populated in the remote Canadian farm town, that off-the-grid community. She wasn't used to so many people crammed into one room. Even a massive ballroom like this. So it was more than just her family that was overwhelming. She was still acclimating to being surrounded by such a sheer number of people.

Sometimes, when she was in Canada, she'd thought she'd dreamed the opulence of her father's Alaskan world. Right now, she saw she hadn't dreamed up a single detail. The Steele family wealth was real. Not a penny had been spared for Delaney's casino-themed engagement party.

As she strolled farther into the party, her eyes were drawn to the intricate details of the Monte Carlo feel. The indicators of unrivaled wealth made this event seem like a scene from a movie. She had vague memories of such lush parties when she'd still lived in Alaska as a child. But her off-the-grid teenage time was a world away from anything of this scale.

Oversize cards with hearts were suspended from the ceiling. Centerpieces of long-stemmed red roses in shiny black vases sat on crisp white tablecloths, which held a collection of discarded drinkware the waitstaff cleared regularly.

Chatter mingled with the thrum of the grand piano, making Brea's heart beat faster. She glanced over her shoulder. Her pearl drop earrings teased along her neck as she eyed the photography station in the corner, with a table full of costume pieces, as well as larger-than-life king and queen of hearts cards with the faces cut out.

Men in tuxedos who were standing with their glittering dates waited in line to have their photos taken. Laughter billowed from the costume-fitting area, where women in designer gowns donned feathered masks and boas or tiaras and faux-fur shawls.

Ward's warm hand palmed her back as they moved deeper into the soiree, past the active roulette table, where a skinny blonde woman excitedly clapped at her winnings. Past the blackjack tables, where important figures of the Alaskan community sat with neutral faces as the pot in the center grew. The blackjack tables captivated some of the Mikkelsons. A woman's voice crooned over the sound system, an A-list celebrity.

Brea stumbled as she caught a glimpse of her twin. Naomi. Her closest sibling hadn't been at the family dinner the other night, which had made things easier, and harder, too.

Suddenly Brea's legs and limbs felt heavy as she studied her sister, who was wearing a rhinestone gown, the skirt black tulle, in a Cinderella poof. But Naomi had always had a flare for the dramatic. Broderick's wife, Glenna, somehow managed to carry off a gold lace dress with a short train of tan feathers.

Brea smoothed her hands down her simple black sheath dress, cinched at the waist with a wide pearl-studded belt. True, she'd felt like an outsider before tonight. But even her level of dress seemed to mark her as different. As someone who didn't belong to this world.

Despite being born into it.

Her stomach dropped thirteen stories. Heat pulsated on her cheeks, and for a moment the world of the party felt distant. Muffled. Underwater.

Until Ward cut through, his hand gently touching her back again.

"Would you like to get something to eat?" He gestured toward the tables of sweets.

On the far wall, Brea spotted cube truffles that were decorated like dice, and a woman in a sequined silver ball gown scooped them onto her crystal plate.

But the real eye-catching feature of the dessert area was a yet-to-be-cut tiered cake that was decorated to resemble a roulette wheel.

"No, thank you. I ate plenty before you picked me up," she lied. Truth be told, the thought of food sent waves of nausea through her. No. Brea's nerves were too electric to keep food down at this point.

"Dance?"

She wanted to, anything to escape speaking with these people. She wasn't ready for this after all. "But aren't you here to work?"

"My presence is enough." He took her hand and pulled her to the dance floor, taking her into his arms.

A welcome haven right now.

"I don't recognize some of the guests." She felt

less conspicuous watching other people from the safety of his embrace.

He nodded toward the front two tables near the mahogany-planked dance floor. "That's the future groom's family. But no one expects you to know everyone."

His fingers were light on her spine. Strangely reassuring and tantalizing at the same time. And a touch that made her more aware than she wanted to admit. "I should though, after my time working for the company, using a fake name."

"You're admitting what you did?" His brows shot up as he and Brea moved to the music. So close. So distracting to be caught up in his strong arms and sexy gaze.

Yet she couldn't deny that being close to him somehow settled her nerves.

She just needed to keep her head on straight and quit thinking with her hormones. She weighed her words carefully. "It's no secret."

"Your lawyer wouldn't be pleased you're talking about it."

"Good point. I guess I was feeling too comfortable around you," she said tightly. "I won't make that mistake again."

A slow smile creased dimples into his cheeks, his hand moving in slow circles along her back. "You're gutsy. Like your twin."

Lord knows she and Naomi had been close as kids, but competitive. She wasn't so sure she wanted that competition now. Even though her sister was married, with twins of her own, and Brea had no business feeling proprietary about Ward. "Is that a compliment?"

"It is. She's respected in the business world."

Business? That was their arrangement. Still… "What about personally?"

"She's tough. So are you," he said simply, his words carrying a weight of emotion. "You've both been through a lot."

Her eyes stung, and she was grateful for the dim lighting that hid the way she was battling back tears. "I barely recognize my own relatives."

She meant that literally and figuratively. She'd lost so much time with her siblings. They'd grown from gangly kids into beautiful and handsome adults. But what threw her the most was the interaction with the Mikkelsons, their once-sworn rivals, in business and in personal affairs.

"Your family has grown now that two families have managed to mesh their immense empires." He pulled her closer as the saxophone let out a wailing, soulful note. Her nostrils filled with the spiciness of his aftershave. Her eyes slid closed for a second before her common sense kicked in and walls went up.

"Managed how? You're the boss. Seems to me that means they failed to mesh very well since an outsider is now at the helm." Nothing about coming home was as she had expected.

"I see it differently." His voice was gravelly as they swayed together, the warmth of him tempting.

A man in a tuxedo, with a gold bowtie, maneuvered past them. A woman in a shimmery turquoise gown with glitzy jewels followed close behind, dancing as she went by, empty champagne glass glinting in the soft light.

"How so?"

The pianist paused, reaching the end of a piece. A dramatic violin joined along with the singer's sultry voice.

"The siblings on both sides have found where they fit best rather than where they were expected to step in. They're now in the places I would have hired them to fill instead of nepotism appointments."

"Are you actually saying that having my brother— Broderick—run Alaska Oil Barons, Inc., would have been a bad choice?"

Ward shrugged his impossibly broad shoulders. "He could have run Steele Enterprises. But the combined Steele and Mikkelson corporations? I'm the stronger CEO to take the helm."

She laughed softly. "It's a shame you don't have any self-confidence."

"This isn't about confidence or arrogance. It's about our resumes and strengths."

Somehow his practicality managed to keep arrogance out of the equation. "I'm glad you're happy with your new job. But what happens when a bigger fish comes along for you?"

"Right now, there isn't a larger company with this

much autonomy. And with me at the helm, Alaska Oil Barons, Inc., *will* grow."

She pressed her head against his chest, his heartbeat echoing softly, steadily against her ear. "I hope that confidence proves to be true."

"For your family's sake."

"Can we talk about something other than business?"

"You aren't angling for your fake job back?"

His accusation stung. "I only pretended to be Milla to get the lay of the land before returning home as myself. That's all."

"Hmm... Maybe you should work for the business."

His touch and gaze had her wits addled. "Whatever for?"

"Your skills at bluffing could be of use to the company in negotiations."

She couldn't decide whether to be complimented or insulted by his words. Then a movement just over Ward's shoulders distracted her.

Naomi crossed the dance floor with Royce, her husband. Naomi's gaze moved past Brea, then back again and she stopped in the middle of dancing couples for a moment.

For a split second, Brea thought they could just pick up where they'd left off, that their twin-sister bond would make everything okay. Then Naomi's face twisted into something that looked an awful lot like suspicion. Her twin's furrowed brow sparked alarm in Brea. The last thing she needed was some residual twin bond giving away her charade.

Brea looped her arms around Ward's neck, and she arched up on her toes to do away with suspicions the best way possible.

She kissed him in full view of all the guests.

Four

Fire scorched through Ward at Brea's kiss.

His senses went on overload at the soft give of her mouth against his, her fingers on his neck, toying with his hairline. His mind flooded with all the ways he wanted to touch her, to explore her gentle curves without the barrier of clothes between them. Not that he could pursue those thoughts or even indulge the kiss to the fullest with so many people around them.

But someday they would share more.

He was determined.

When the time and place was right, he would kiss every inch of her beautiful body.

With a final skim of his lips over hers, he eased

back, taking in the heat in her molten dark eyes. "Damn, lady, you take my breath away."

"You're a smooth talker," she said skeptically, but he could see that her pulse still raced, throbbing along her neck.

"I'm actually better known for being a blunt speaker of truth." Which was important for her to know.

If she couldn't be trusted, she needed to know where he stood. And if she was being truthful and was a victim, then she needed to know he was a straight shooter.

"Since the pianist is taking a break," he said, "let's get something to drink and have a seat. We can talk."

She nodded, her pupils still wide with desire. With a tender hand trailing down her spine and resting on the small of her back, Ward guided her past the partiers. She seemed to sigh into his touch, the muscles melting with his caresses. A reaction that made his heart hammer with impatience. Anticipation.

As they rounded the roulette table, a bevy of applause erupted. The crowd moved around a blonde in her midfifties. Even from across the room, he would know that glittering silhouette anywhere. The gap in the crowd revealed Jeannie Mikkelson standing cross-armed in a jade-green sequined ball gown, talking to her youngest son. Brea's neck snapped to attention, and he felt the tension return to her. Could see the unease work upward from her low back to her shoulders. Knew her nerves must be fraying. Knew he had to take action.

Ward steered her toward the quieter corridor. On his way, he snagged two glasses of champagne. Echoes of music from the grand piano drifted with them down the hall. The casino theme continued— larger-than-life cards with hearts flanked the walls. And there, in front of them, was the quietest Steele of all the siblings and the woman of the hour, Delaney Steele.

Brea backed up a step.

Delaney's spiral-curled hair bounced as she took a step forward. Her smile was as bright as the crystals that edged the bodice of her fitted black dress.

"Hello, Breanna," Delaney said gently. "Thank you for coming to my engagement party. It means so much to me."

A slow swallow moved down Brea's throat. She nodded toward her sister's left hand, which sported a pear-shaped diamond ring. "That's lovely."

"Thank you. I'm just happy to be marrying the love of my life." She smiled. "Like Naomi, you and I dreamed of when we were kids, dressing up for weddings with a towel for a veil."

Ward inched aside, giving them space, but keeping his gaze on Brea's face, gauging her reactions. He hadn't considered until now that having her spend more time with her family was perhaps the best way to get to the bottom of her reasons for returning after she'd revealed herself as Milla Jones. Sure Shana

Mikkelson's private-eye skills had uncovered Brea's locale, but with the skills she had from living off-the-grid, she could have disappeared. Instead she'd gotten a lawyer and come back to Alaska.

To what end?

"I want to trust you all." Brea's legs folded, and she sat on the velvet settee. "But it's so difficult to figure out what's real in my memories, good and bad."

"If you have any questions, I'm happy to help however I can. I *want* to help." Delaney sat beside her, resting a hand on Brea's arm, her engagement ring catching the chandelier lights. "You don't need to tell me any details of that memory. You could just ask something, like 'family vacation to the Gold Rush festival when we were in elementary school.' I'll tell you what I remember. You can decide if it matches up with what you recall."

Brea's eyes widened in surprise. "That's a good idea. Maybe we can try it sometime next week."

"Or you could ask me something now."

Brea hesitated, then shook her head. "This is your engagement party. I don't want to monopolize you when you should be celebrating your dreams coming true."

"You're family." Delaney waved a dismissive hand, her engagement ring glinting. "And having the chance to talk to you is a joy I never thought I would have again."

Ward leaned forward in the chair. No one had asked him to leave and he didn't plan to offer. He couldn't deny the protective urge to stay near Brea. And as much as he reminded himself of his uncertainty about trusting her, bottom line, he had to make sure she wasn't hurt by whatever her sister had to say about their childhood memories.

Brea nodded. "Okay then. Tell me about Saturday-morning breakfasts."

Delaney's smile spread wide and fast. "I remember all sorts of special times at Kit's Kodiak Café. But my favorite memory is the morning we shared a candy bracelet…"

Delaney Steele looked forward to going to Kit's Kodiak Café with her dad and her brothers and her sisters while their mom had a morning all to herself.

Today was special. She got to sit next to Brea. Brea liked to sit at the end, and Naomi usually sat beside her, since they were twins. But this morning, Delaney had run so fast into the restaurant that she almost slipped on the ice. But she made it.

She had Brea all to herself.

Well, sort of. Everyone was talking so much, Delaney couldn't get a word in edgewise. Well, everyone except for Marshall. He was quiet, reading a book about horses. If he didn't have his nose in a book, he was in the stables.

Delaney swung her legs back and forth, her feet not reaching the ground. She loved this place. It wasn't fancy. She felt comfortable. The diner looked like a big barn near the water. The windows showed a pretty view of a dock stretching out into the lake. Inside, long-planked tables were set up for big, noisy groups—like her family.

Menus crackled in front of the others, but she knew what she wanted off the Three Polar Bears menu. Pancakes and reindeer sausage.

Usually she was impatient to get her food. But today she was content to wait. Besides, their family was well known in this café and they'd be served quickly. But their dad always said not to ask for special treatment.

She and her siblings had been coming to Kit's for as long as Delaney could remember. Their father brought them most Saturday mornings and even sometimes before school so their mom could have a break. He would bundle them up. He wasn't good at remembering to match up everyone's gloves and hats. But they were all warm. Even if Marshall was mad over wearing a pink kitten hat.

Her mom told her once that their dad, who had more money than anyone, was trying to keep them grounded by taking them to regular sorts of places, the kinds that played country music and oldies over the radio. The air smelled of home cooking and a wood fire. The stuffed bear was a little scary, but she didn't want to admit to being afraid.

Delaney tapped Brea's leg with her foot. Her sister looked over, frowning. "What?"

"Shhh," Delaney said softly and held her hand out under the table.

She'd brought an extra candy bracelet, just in case she got to sit by Brea. Delaney had used her allowance to buy it. She kept her hand out of sight, though, so her dad couldn't see and say they were going to wreck their appetites.

But no amount of candy could make her too full for Kit's Kodiak food.

Brea smiled. "Thanks, kiddo."

Kiddo? She was only three years younger. But Delaney had a tough time standing up for herself. It was easier to stand up for others. Like how she'd done a report on saving the whales at school even though the mean girls made fun of her at lunch and called her whale girl. Not that she told her family. She didn't want to make things tougher for her parents.

Their dad always said their mom had the hardest job of all, dealing with the Steele hellions, and the least he could do was give her a break sometimes. He'd rolled out that speech at the start of every breakfast and reminded them to listen to their mom and their teachers. If there were no bad reports, then they could all go fishing with him. Fishing was so fun, they didn't even tattle on each other. They figured things out on their own when they argued.

She and her siblings had a tight bond. She couldn't imagine what life would be like without her family. Just thinking about it made her stomach hurt so much she passed the rest of her candy bracelet to her sister...

* * *

Back at her apartment, after the engagement party, Brea wasn't sure if she felt better or worse hearing her sister tell her story about that breakfast morning so long ago, when Delaney had shared her candy bracelet.

Brea's emotions were all jumbled up. A dangerous state as she stood in her apartment entryway with Ward. He'd insisted on walking her to her door. With that kiss on the dance floor still fresh in her mind—and tingling along her senses—she wasn't sure it was wise to be alone with him.

Not that she didn't trust him. He hadn't pushed faster than she was ready.

But she didn't trust herself.

The draw to him had grown stronger than ever tonight. It was getting tougher and tougher to resist him and the undeniable chemistry between them. But she needed to remember he was loyal first and foremost to her father, to the Steeles, to the company.

Still, her memory churned with thoughts of his hand on her back at the party, steadying her when she'd needed it. Helping her make a graceful exit when she'd been tongue-tied after Delaney's story.

Her emotions were a jumble.

She needed an outlet, and the man in front of her was one sexy, welcome distraction.

As he stepped from the apartment building hallway into her entry, he tucked his gloves into the pockets of his long black wool coat. She closed the

door and he unbuttoned the coat to reveal his tai-
lored tux. Still, he didn't move any deeper into her
apartment.

Neither had she.

He took her hand in his, his thumb rubbing along
the inside of her wrist. "Are you okay?"

"Of course. I only had two glasses of champagne,"
she answered, deliberately dodging the obvious reason he asked.

"I meant are you all right with what your sister
said. You've been quiet."

Nerves threatened to return, and she forced something that felt like a smile to her lips. But her lips wavered as words formed. "I was shouting *gargoyle* in
my head."

His forehead creased with concern. "I apologize.
I should have been paying closer attention—"

"That was a joke." Brea squeezed his hand, his
strength and calluses launching a fresh wash of tingles through her.

He shook his head. "What's happened to you and
your family is indescribable and not at all material
for humor."

"I'm working on my attitude." She kept her hand
in his, the warmth of his touch grounding her and
exciting her all at once. "Although, somehow I'm still
telling lies about us being in a relationship."

Ward shifted his weight, and she caught a whiff
of his spicy cologne and his own musk as the floor-

board beneath him creaked. "Your life has been…confusing."

Understatement of the year.

Brea took a deep breath, her mind racing back to certain touchstones of her complicated existence.

"After my foster parents died, I had my own sort of off-the-grid lifestyle."

Ward's strong fingers offered her palms a massage. He looked at her with those deep blue eyes. "I'd like to hear more."

"I spent some time on my own in Canada, doing jobs for cash. Learning about how the world worked. Trying to figure out where my head was at, trying to figure out what I wanted to do about my…relatives."

Her blood relations, as well as her adoptive ones. She'd wrestled with reconciling her feelings for everyone. She'd grieved when her adoptive parents died, as had their small community. But then when she'd come across a box under her mom's bed, her world had tipped.

The box had contained the clothes she'd been wearing that day of the plane crash, along with a mermaid Beanie Baby that her grandmother had given her. The memory of that simple present had made her realize there was no more hiding from the truth.

She needed to go back to see her Steele relatives.

If only her brain didn't still push back every time she tried to analyze those walled-away years.

"So you snuck into the company."

She recoiled from his touch for a moment. Her

hands to her temples, shaking her head and squeezing her eyes shut. "It doesn't make complete sense now. I didn't know who to trust for advice on what would be the best way to approach them." She shrugged. "I'm here now."

"And they hadn't come looking for you?"

"I would have come back in my own time, as myself. I came here in disguise, on my own, didn't I? I just feel this…reunion isn't something to rush." Her mind was a jumble of thoughts from those teenage years. There was so much, too much, to process. She wanted life to be simple for once. "You're not one to cast stones on role-play for a goal. You're pretending to be my boyfriend."

"I could be your for-real lover. Our chemistry is off the charts. Just say the word and we can pursue that."

His eyes danced with a dangerous anticipation she felt echoing in her blood. In the restless pounding of her heart. In the small step she took toward him.

The scent of the lavender potpourri in a dish in the foyer relaxed her even as the scent of his aftershave tempted her closer. Leaning toward him slightly, her voice dropped a notch, her words breathy, her pulse speeding twice as fast as the soft ticking of the clock. "And that word would be?"

"Let's have sex? Or let's go out to dinner? Or how about both?"

Awareness crackled between them, her skin tingling. The heat built to a desire that wiped away the confusion and grief she'd been battling since her sister shared that heart-tugging memory that matched Brea's recollection to the letter.

She needed, craved, a respite from the tension. She wanted to feel the love of this family again, but she was scared if she let her guard down enough to let that happen, she could be opening her heart to a hurt she wouldn't recover from. The tension of it—the wanting and wishing for an acceptance she wasn't ready to take—was draining. And it hurt. But with Ward touching her this way, she knew she could put her worries aside for a few hours in his arms. And with the heat simmering in his eyes, his touch stirring her inside, she really, really wanted to lose herself with him.

"And there's nothing to say we can't turn this into a real affair. Just say when." She walked her fingers up his chest to smooth his lapels.

"When," he growled, clasping her hands. "Absolutely when."

His mouth met hers again, the kiss deepening in the way it couldn't in public at the party. And oh my, the man knew how to kiss, fully, his whole attention on her and turning her inside out with the stroke of his tongue and his hands over her clothes…then under. The rasp of his calluses along her tender flesh was a sweet temptation.

A sigh whispered between her lips.

Her restless fingers swept off his overcoat, and

then his tuxedo jacket, before tugging at his tie. She couldn't get him undressed fast enough.

"So, Ward Benally," she said, her voice husky, "are you sure I'm not taking advantage of you? Because I wouldn't want you to do anything you don't want to do."

"If you are taking advantage of me, keep on going."

She angled back to see if he was teasing her. "Benally…"

"Trust me, I want you, Breanna Steele. Absolutely. Fully. Here and now. Soon, or I'm going to lose my mind." He growled his chuckle and appreciation.

And she was happy to keep up the pace until his shirt and T were gone, her hips pressed against his, the impressive length of his erection a promise she eagerly anticipated.

He turned her around to pull the zipper down her back, exposing her spine an inch at a time, kissing along the bared skin until she was a quivering mass of need. Her feet shaking, she faced him again, easing the dress down, slowly, savoring the passion and appreciation in his gaze as the dress pooled around her feet.

Emboldened, she stood before him, wearing nothing but a satin strapless bra and matching panties. And by the looks of his erection, which strained against his fly, this sexy man was every bit as turned on looking at her as she was by looking at him. Knowing he wanted her as much as she craved this time with him made her head swim.

Her fingers connected with his chest and static snapped. A tingle radiated up her arm. She reached out again, her touch connecting this time, and she trailed lower, lower still, until she slid her hand into his tuxedo pants.

His eyes slid closed and his head fell back as she stroked, learning the feel of him, anticipating what was to come. His chest expanded with a deep sigh. "We need to move this to the bedroom."

"Or the sofa is closer." She arched up on her toes to kiss him again.

"Hold that thought for one second." He knelt to reach into his jacket…and pulled out a condom. Thank goodness at least one of them was thinking clearly enough to take care of birth control.

Then he returned to her, and her thoughts scattered, instinct taking over.

Their legs tangled as they made their way from the hall to the sofa, leaving a trail of his shoes and her heels. She caressed his pants down his legs. His hands made fast work of her bra and panties.

Flesh to flesh, they tumbled back onto the sofa in a tangle. She nipped along his strong jaw, the leather cushion soft against her back, his touch gentle along her sides.

The thick pressure of him between her legs almost sent her over the edge then and there. Her breath hitched. He thrust deep and full, holding while she adjusted to the newness of him, of them linked.

She arched into the sensation, taking him deeper

inside, savoring the connection she'd dreamt of since she had first met him. Being with him was everything she'd hoped—even more. It was chemistry like none she'd experienced before.

And she wanted more.

He held his weight off her with one hand on the back of the couch. She rolled her hips under his and he took the cue, resuming the dance they'd started earlier. Her fingernails dug half-moons into his shoulders, urgency pulsing through her.

She buried her face against his neck, breathing in the scent of his aftershave. He kissed, nipped and laved his way to her breast, his five-o'clock shadow rasped against her sensitive skin.

Passion ramping higher, hotter, she wrapped her legs around his waist and writhed, nearly sliding from the sofa. But he caught her, steadied her, secured her. His eyes held hers as firmly as his hands. His expression challenged her, encouraged her.

He seemed so in control, it gave her pause. Until she looked closer and saw tendons straining in his neck with restraint. His pleasure pleased her. His gravelly voice filled the air with all the times he'd watched and wanted her as he slid his hand between them. He circled his thumb with just the right skill to take her to the edge, and then he eased back again. Then...

Bliss.

Her release shimmered through her, pulling a cry of pleasure from her with each ripple of her orgasm.

He braced his hand against the sofa back and thrust into her, once, twice more. His completion echoed hers, sending more shimmers through her until she was limp in the aftermath.

Somehow he managed to stand. He scooped her up and carried her to the bedroom. He eased her onto the comforter and stretched out beside her, tugging a pink quilt up from the foot of the bed. He pulled her close and stroked her hair, his touch gentle.

She kept her gaze from his, not ready to let him see the vulnerability she knew he would find in her eyes. Instead she focused on the glass lamp.

He was too perceptive, and she feared he would see the truth of how much he'd affected her. How she'd never felt this level of intensity before, and she wasn't sure how to handle the feelings he stirred.

Inhaling the scent of lavender that wafted from her oil diffuser, she attempted to bring herself back down to something more grounded. Something less dangerous than the feel of her body pressed to his.

She was in way over her head.

She had gone into this to escape from her confusing feelings about her family, but now she had a whole fresh batch of tender feelings to deal with, and this time those emotions had Ward's name on them. She didn't know where to put all of the rawness she felt, but she already wanted to be with him again. And if she wasn't careful, she would throw caution to the wind, which would leave her defenseless. Something she vowed never to be again.

* * *

Sitting on a barstool in Brea's kitchen, wearing only his boxers, Ward felt like he'd time traveled back to his marriage.

Which was the last thought he wanted to be having right now with the scent of Brea still on him, with the rush of their incredible sex still humming through his veins.

He wanted this affair with her. He deserved it, damn it.

And except for their morning coziness, it was *nothing* like his marriage.

Through sheer force of will, he shoved back memories of his broken marriage and lost child. The here and now was all that counted for him. His job. This moment with an incredibly sexy woman.

A woman with whom he also needed to keep his wits about him.

Beside him, Brea fluffed her long, dark hair. Slicing through his thoughts with the way his tuxedo shirt rolled up along her thighs, hinting at the curves of her bottom. She'd made a sangria blend from wine and fruit, serving it with avocado slices, shrimp and chips. Working beside her to prepare the snack had been easy and intimate.

A bit too close to domesticity for his peace of mind. And from the looks of her, she was as uncomfortable as he was.

He rested a hand on her knee. "I don't regret what we did."

She gave a shaky breath. "I don't either. It was just more intense than I expected. Apparently, I'm no good at casual sex."

He hadn't expected such an honest response from her. "We are fake dating." Even though they were most definitely having real sex. He squeezed her knee, smiling. "That's a step beyond casual."

"Okay, I can see that." She gave him a wry smile. "Thank you for not taking my words as some kind of request that you get down on one knee and propose." Brea scooped up an avocado slice and a piece of shrimp onto a blue corn tortilla chip and popped it into her mouth absentmindedly.

Her words chilled him. "Not a chance. Been there. Done that. Bear the battle scars."

"Because of your daughter?"

Brea's knee brushed his. The touch brought a mixture of exciting newness and a past that haunted him.

"My stepdaughter," he reminded her. "I thought a person got married, and the rest fell into place over time. I was in love with my wife. I loved her kid— thought of Paisley as my own child. We were going to be a family."

"What happened to Paisley's biological father?" She brought the strawberry to her lips. Bit into it and watched him thoughtfully. Intensely.

He swallowed another swig of wine. "He died before she was born. Paisley thought of me as her dad." And that stabbed clean through him. "She thinks I abandoned her."

"Oh, Ward, that's so sad. Is that what her mom told her?"

Silence pressed on him for a moment. The weight nearly stifled his next words. The reality and truth they spoke.

"She told her she has a new dad, and that I wasn't her real father."

"I'm so very sorry—for you and for Paisley."

"People tell me kids are resilient." He drew in a shaky breath, his memory echoing with Paisley crying when he said goodbye. He reached for a blue corn tortilla chip. Pressed it into his palm until it broke into two. Then he scooped the avocado and shrimp onto one of the pieces and chewed thoughtfully.

Brea nodded, quiet for so long, he wasn't sure she'd speak again. He waited, letting her find her pace.

"That may be true. But it wasn't true for me." She frowned down into her glass. "Maybe I should have told you otherwise."

Again, she'd offered more openness than he'd expected.

"I appreciate that you're honest. I hate being lied to."

"Me, too. The truth is confusing enough without having to sift through deceit."

He stroked her hair back, tucking it behind her ear. "Then let's agree that no matter what else is going on, we'll be honest with each other."

She bit her bottom lip, looking away for a moment

before continuing, "You can't think we're going to tell each other everything?"

His Spider-Sense went off.

What was she hiding?

Even as he wondered, given how closed off she'd become so fast, he knew his chance of getting her to say it was next to nil. "I don't think any man wants to talk that much."

"Okay then." Brea took a delicate sip of sangria, smiling as the glass touched her lips. The dark red wine deliciously stained her mouth. Drawing him in again.

She gave him the laugh he'd hoped for, some of the tension easing from her shoulders.

But it didn't do much to quiet his questions; in particular, the need to know what Brea was hiding that made her so wary. And he couldn't escape the niggling sense that he was focusing on what she was hiding to keep from thinking, from feeling, all the things she made him think and feel.

He damn well wasn't going to put his heart on the line ever again.

Five

Brea couldn't sleep.

She didn't regret having sex with Ward. She did, however, regret that she couldn't just enjoy the aftermath of lazing next to him in a haze of post-sex bliss. Judging by the pounding of her heart, the window of such utter contentment had firmly closed.

She wanted to be with him again.

Too much. Desire pounded through her. So much, she needed to reestablish her equilibrium before facing him again.

Making love to Ward had set her senses ablaze, made everything more vibrant. Even her mind was firing on all cylinders, which made her think of the past. Or rather, both of her pasts. Her life seemed sliced into two parts—before and after the plane crash that took her mother's life.

Brea sat at the kitchen island, laptop open in front of her. She'd been searching the internet for the past few hours. The quest gave her something to distract her from how much she wanted to crawl back under the sheets. Each breath she took drew in the scent of him lingering on his shirt, which she still wore.

Focus, she admonished herself. For so long she'd searched for clues about the accident—about what might have caused it, about who might have been involved—but it was like searching for a needle in a haystack.

Today's quest involved looking into aircraft-maintenance records. Her research quest wasn't exactly a sanctioned one. But she was afraid if the wrong person learned she was still prying, they would destroy any leads to what happened all those years ago.

She studied the aircraft reports in front of her, losing herself in the monotony of page after page that had been scanned into digital files. She knew Tally Benson—soon to be Steele—was related to the mechanic who'd worked on the aircraft. But there had been a number of others who'd worked on the aircraft or had been involved with the flight. Even though Tally had told everyone about her father's connection, it still seemed surreal for her to now be a part of the family in spite of that connection. Even though the crash wasn't the woman's fault, how could the

Steeles look at Tally and not think of what her dad had done?

Brea wondered if she too was a reminder of what had happened, what the family had lost.

What someone had wanted to destroy but had failed.

And if someone harbored feelings of guilt or vengeance, wouldn't those feelings be magnified by Brea's presence?

Scanning her gaze along the photos lining the mantel, she felt something tug at her subconscious. Something she needed to pull into the forefront and examine. But her memories about that day were as clear as mist.

She'd never been able to bring into sharp focus the events of the twenty-four hours surrounding the crash, the terrifying images too laden with her emotions for her to sift down to the facts underneath. Afterward, when she'd gone to her adoptive family for answers, their accounts had swayed her strongly. They'd told her that her Alaskan family was no good, that they had given up on her. That they were corrupt. She was better off without them. And even knowing that the couple who had claimed to love her for her entire teenage life had been lying to her, she still couldn't bring herself to trust the Steeles.

It was ironic that while she'd been with her adoptive parents, she'd mistrusted her biological family. And now she was finding it tougher to believe in the people who'd taken her in, her perspective tilting completely. It was enough to drive a person mad.

The tingly sense of being watched had her sitting up straight and fast. So fast, she nearly toppled the barstool at the island. She turned to find Ward standing in the bedroom doorway, watching her.

His boxers hung low on his lean hips, drawing her eyes to his washboard abs, then lower. Her mind flooded with memories of the passionate way they'd tangled in the sheets and all the sensual things she still wanted to experience with him. They could find that bliss again, if she let herself.

He combed his fingers through his rumpled hair. "What're you working on?"

Ice chilled her heated blood. She swiveled on the barstool, back to her computer, rapidly shutting down the screen. How could she have forgotten what she was doing? And why had she allowed herself to be so reckless as to research the Mikkelson and Steele families while Ward was under her roof?

She slammed the lid closed. "Just, um, checking emails and researching articles on relaxation and meditation to see if it can help me sift through the memories of my past. Hearing Delaney talk about childhood memories was really helpful."

The lies rolled off her tongue with an ease that made her uncomfortable, especially so soon after discussing being honest with each other. But she'd realized she would never find the answers she sought if she didn't circumvent the truth on occasion. She didn't enjoy lying, but it was a means to an end.

She also knew those fibs needed to have something with teeth, something with an element of truth. In this scenario, Delaney had been helpful in confirming her confusion and mistrust.

"That's a good idea." He strode closer to her, his steps silent, like a lean tiger's. "Any interesting emails?"

Very. Including one from a lady who'd worked at a local airport around the time of the crash. Not that Brea intended to tell him that. Instead she settled on sharing another email. "My family—the Steeles—want me to come to lunch tomorrow. Delaney told them how well our discussion about the childhood memories went."

"Are you sure it's wise to push that hard?" Blue eyes shone as he gave Brea's hand a squeeze. The touch passed fire between them even now.

There was no rule book for this sort of situation. She hadn't meant for her life to grow so enmeshed with Ward's, but what had started as a fake relationship had surprised her by giving her an outlet for the intense stress she'd encountered while digging for answers. Now she could only move forward and try to make the best of her situation.

She was in too deep to turn back now.

"I don't think it's wise to bury my head in the sand and assume all will work out." Which she'd done in the months after her adoptive parents had died. She'd

packed up a couple of trunks full of belongings—
books they'd read together on long winter nights,
crafts they'd made, a dress she'd worn to a high school
dance and, of course, that fateful shoebox she'd opened
later to find her few surviving belongings from the
day of the crash. "The only way to know who to trust
is to get to know my family better. So yes, I want to
go to lunch."

To learn more.

Information was power.

"What would your counselor say?"

She appreciated his concern, but his coddling?
Not so much. She needed her independence, to learn
to trust her instincts again. "That I should trust my
instincts more when it comes to taking charge of
my life."

That was easier said than done. She wanted evidence. Tangible truths.

He rested a hand on top of her computer. "What
do you think you should do right now?"

Find out if he'd seen anything. But if he had, then
she might have to push him away. And she couldn't
scrounge for the will to do that when she wanted
more than anything to lean into all that sexy strength
and warmth. She couldn't deny herself the pleasure
of spending more time with a man who captivated
her so thoroughly. He chased all her muddled memories and confusion away. She might well have to
leave this town one day. Before that time came, she
intended to make the most of every moment with

him. The past would have to stay in the past for a few hours.

"My gut says we should go back into the bedroom, and you should give me a thorough massage before we go back to bed for a few hours." She stroked the toes of one foot along the side of his calf. "In the interest of relaxing, of course."

A slow smile spread across his face as he lifted her off the barstool and into his arms. "You should follow those instincts more often."

Ward had never given anyone a massage before. But he fully intended to do so again—if the person happened to be Brea.

Their hours of sex had been mind-bending. Even now, the next day and a shower later, his senses were still saturated with the sweet taste and floral scent of her. Not to mention the creamy feel of her skin under his hands.

Of course those were dangerous thoughts to have while standing in the stables with her father. But Ward was here to learn more about the man who'd founded such an impressive oil dynasty.

And of course there was Ward's affair with Brea. A long-lost daughter Jack might feel overprotective of, with good reason, after all she'd been through.

It was more important than ever that Ward keep his wits around this man. He didn't know Jack Steele all that well—something that needed to change.

It seemed quite clear that Jack loved his kids,

though. But what about his dead wife? Could the man have had something to do with her death, and he'd never meant Brea to be in harm's way? The man had made a marriage to the business enemy. Some might see that as mighty Machiavellian. And while not so long ago, he would have taken pride in that, now he wasn't so sure.

Brea was getting to him in more ways than he could count, and although he needed to keep his eyes on her, that proximity also made objectivity tougher.

Ward definitely intended to keep a close eye on Jack Steele, for Brea's sake.

Leather cowboy boots punching through the hard, packed snow, Ward moved into the barn. Bits of hay were scattered on the ground surrounding an onyx-colored horse that Jack had clipped to the crossties.

Stetson tipped back on his dark head, and Jack crouched down, examining the horse's back left hoof. The Friesian's eyes were rimmed with white. Clearly nervous.

Looking over his shoulder, Jack cradled the hoof with his leg and hand. Motioned for Ward to approach. "Meet Flash—our newest rescue. She's a little skittish. Owners abandoned her in a stall when their ranch got foreclosed on. Bridlebrook Rescue got to her in time. Thankfully. Put some meat back on her bones. We took her in yesterday."

Ward reached out to touch the mare's flowing

black mane. As he touched her neck, Flash lowered her head down. Eyes growing soft. A sigh escaped.

Jack smiled. "That's a good sign. She's a nervous thing, but we're going to work on rehabilitating her spirits. And—" Jack glanced down at the semi-swollen hoof "—healing this abscess."

Nodding absently, Ward was hit between the eyes with a memory. For a moment, a life Ward never got to live flashed through his brain. Once he had imagined getting a horse for Paisley. Teaching her how to ride. How to care for a horse. How to notice the start of an abscess or colic. He could practically hear her crystalline laughter as he imagined her learning to canter and barrel race.

The almost-memory cut him deep and true before Jack's movement beside him brought him back to the barn.

Jack touched the frog of the horse's foot, assessing the abscess before bringing his deep blue eyes to meet Ward's. "What brings you here, Benally?"

With an effort, he breathed out the ache of losing his daughter. Focused instead on why he came.

"Your daughter's having lunch with the family. I came along with her." Not exactly a lie. Not exactly the truth. He found himself quickly returning to his night with Brea. He craved that again. A dangerous feeling. Damn it, he was getting too emotionally involved with her, wanting to help her family.

"Brea actually showed up?" Jack straightened,

his face surprised and vulnerable in a way that Ward doubted many people had ever seen. "Thank you."

His hand rested on Flash's hindquarters. The mare kept weight off her injured hoof.

"She makes her own choices. She's strong-willed, like her father."

Jack relaxed into a nostalgic smile. "You should have met her mom."

He wished he had. What might Brea be like today if her mother hadn't died in a tragic accident that involved her, too? The crash, her mother's death and the loss of the rest of her family had all defined her in so many ways.

Ward stayed silent as Jack returned to Flash.

Jack felt the tendons along Flash's leg. "How're you liking the new office?"

"The job is an exciting challenge. We're going to make great things happen for the company, which will expand the reach of your family's new charitable organization, as well. There are good things on the horizon."

Damn, he sounded like a PR piece. He extended a hand for Flash to sniff. He kept his palm open as the horse's muzzle blew hot air into his hand. The horse relaxed even more.

Jack swept off his Stetson and wiped a wrist over his forehead wearily. "This isn't the way I saw things playing out when we decided to merge the companies."

"You wanted your son at the helm. I get that."

And Broderick Steele probably would have made a solid choice for the position, except he no longer had the killer instinct.

"Or Jeannie's son."

"Really?" Ward asked in surprise as Flash let out a nicker.

"Maybe…" Jack nodded, seeming earnest enough. "But…"

"But not some stranger like me," Ward finished the older man's sentence.

"You're a top-notch choice," Jack said diplomatically. "I understand we're lucky to have you."

Ward noticed Jack still hadn't admitted to being okay about the way things had turned out. But the guy had bigger concerns now, which could also account for his lack of ire. Clearly Ward wasn't going to find out anything about Jack's feelings for his dead wife. Could there be valid reasons for Brea's suspicions? "I guess I should head back in for lunch. Which is the reason I came out here. Jeannie says they're ready to serve."

Jack gripped his arm, stopping him. "Do you really care for my daughter?"

"Whoa, don't start looking at me as a future son-in-law." Ward tried to pass off the conversation as lighthearted but found no humor in the man's blue eyes. "No disrespect. We're just dating."

"I wasn't renting a church hall. Just curious." Jack turned over the hoof pick in his hands. Metal glinting in the barn light. "She's still so closed up when talking to me."

"I'm sorry, sir." And Ward was.

The older man's words struck a chord. Ward understood what it was like to lose a child. While his daughter hadn't died, he'd been cut out of her life, and that hurt like hell every day. It was an ever-present knot in his chest that, on most days, threatened to crack his rib cage.

Jack cleared his throat. "She's here. She's alive. I can be patient as long as I know she's okay and I can see her. That's so much more than I ever imagined."

Ward couldn't even wrap his brain around how Jack Steele must have felt, believing his daughter had died.

That kind of pain was inconceivable. Suddenly the whole fake relationship with Brea stung Ward's conscience…except in some ways, it wasn't fake anymore.

They were lovers, for however long that lasted.

He needed to tread warily with the family patriarch.

"Jack, your respect means a lot to me. I'm doing my best to earn your trust."

"As the head of the company or as my daughter's boyfriend?"

"Both," Ward said, because there really wasn't another answer to give.

Too fast, Brea was filling his thoughts, and that could be dangerous for a man who'd vowed to make

business his life. He'd seen his personal life go up
in smoke once before, and he had no intention of
repeating that mistake.

Brea regretted not signing up for meditative-yoga
classes back when she'd lived in Canada. She could
have really used the training on how to be mindful
when her life felt out of control. To understand how to
use her breath to quiet down her galloping thoughts
and racing heart.

She could add it to a list of things she needed
to accomplish. Skills to acquire to make it through
this fractured life that was still so full of shards and
questions.

A life that felt strangely surreal as she sat in the
great room of Marshall's home, formerly the Steele
home, where she'd spent much of her life as a small
child.

The towering ceiling and the railing around the
upstairs hallway was so familiar—rustic luxury. Not
that such a familiarity put her at ease or clarified a
thing.

Fat leather chairs and sofas filled the expansive,
light-filled room. She'd curled up in those chairs
many times to read.

Rafters soared upward, dotted with skylights, as
well as lantern-style lights for the long winter nights
with her siblings, mother and grandmother.

One stone wall held a fireplace crackling with
flames. Antlers hung above the mantel. The granite-

slab wet bar overflowed with snacks and drinks. Voices hummed in the great room past the open French doors, leading into the main part of the house.

And outside the glass walls was the most familiar part of all.

She took a deep breath. Counted to three on the inhale. Pushed the exhale slowly out through her nose as memories surged forward.

How had breathing become so difficult?

Chunks of ice breaking loose in the water caused the family seaplane to bob. Her dad had taken her fishing in those waters. He'd insisted his girls bait their own hooks.

She could see tracks where others had ridden earlier today. And in the distance, she could swear she spotted a tree house just like the one she and her siblings had used as children. Her heart squeezed.

So many memories here, in this place.

She let memories roll over her, unprompted. Her uncle helping her onto a paint horse, teaching her where to place her weight in the saddle. Her twin sister's peal of laughter and whispered secrets. Brea knew better than to let her eyes linger on Naomi, the toughest one of all to forget.

Losing her family had been hard, but losing her twin had felt like a limb had gone missing. On so many nights, she'd gone to sleep, seeking that connection twins had, reaching out to Naomi in her mind, convinced that Naomi would know somehow that Brea lived. A childish thought, maybe. But it had persisted well into adulthood.

Had her sister felt that same crippling sense of loss?

Silence stretched as Brea sat alone for the moment, taking in the view, this pristine beauty that stole her breath as fast as the man walking out of the barn and back toward the house.

So much had stayed the same, but the most important things had changed. The people.

It was still surreal seeing her siblings grown-up when they'd stayed frozen as young in what memories she'd retained, those images superimposing over anything she'd managed to find on the computer when she could sneak a search during unsupervised time.

"Hello?" A deep voice carried over her, one she didn't recognize. She barely recognized the face of her youngest brother. He hadn't even been in preschool when she'd…left.

She remembered carrying him on her hip, walking around the house with him like a baby doll in her arms.

"Hello, Aiden. I thought you were off working in the oil fields."

"I got time off to see you." He strode into the room, looking more like a lumberjack than her baby brother. He must be pushing twenty years old now, his hair dark and thick like all of theirs.

"You probably don't remember me." The words

tumbled out of her lips even as the statement cut through her.

"I do—a little anyway. And Dad had us watch videos of you and Mom so we wouldn't forget." Aiden offered a small smile.

It was so strange to see him older without having watched him grow up. But that smile…she would recognize it anywhere. It was their mother's smile. He carried that with him even after having lost her when he was so young.

"I should probably watch those videos." It would be painful, but could also be helpful to have visual confirmation of her memories.

"Dad would like that."

"Tell me something you remember on your own." She found herself making the request before she could second-guess herself. Hearing things from Delaney's point of view had been gut-wrenching but authentic.

Aiden dropped to sit in front of the fire, his shoulders broad in a green flannel shirt. "Well, I remember winter camping in one of those glass igloos. It wasn't cold, and the stars were awesome."

The vision of the past was so vibrant, the memories almost stung. She remembered doing that more than once, the tradition stretching back to before Aiden was born. Had things been as idyllic as they sounded? Or was it all a re creation of moments perfected for video?

She glanced outside again, at Ward, wondering if

what she felt with him was as intense as it seemed
or only heightened because of how upside down her
life was. And was he with her because he was looking for some sense of family after losing his?

She stayed quiet, letting her youngest brother talk.

"At night, before bed, our mom sang some song
about a bear cub chasing the Northern Lights across
the sky. I thought I was that little cub."

Brea remembered the night-light that simulated
the same scene, but the rest was tougher to pull free
from the tangle in her head.

Aiden stood, dusting off his jeans. "I hope I didn't
make you feel uncomfortable."

"We're okay. It's important to get to the bottom
of this. Important for all of us."

"It would mean the world to Dad."

She bit her lip, the ache of what was in the past
being almost too much to bear. She didn't want to
break down and cry in front of him. "I don't want to
monopolize you. I'm sure everyone is eager to visit
with you, too."

"Well, I am sorta dating Alayna Mikkelson."

"Really?" This family just got more and more tangled up, with her dad marrying a Mikkelson. Then
her older brother Broderick marrying one, too. And
now Aiden?

"It's still pretty new, and we're figuring it out." He
shrugged. "She's been having a rough time lately—
something about thinking she saw her uncle stalk-

ing around. Apparently he's a real loser—a drinker and drug addict."

Alarms went off in her head. "Is the uncle a Mikkelson? I thought Charles Mikkelson Sr., was an only child."

"It's their mom's brother. Jeannie's brother."

Somehow that made it more chilling. But Brea didn't want to tell Aiden as much when all she had to go on was her hunches.

"Thank you for talking to me and sharing what you remember about our past. The memories from you and the others are helpful." Even if they made her sad.

Even if seeing her dad made her apprehensive, like she was betraying her adoptive parents. Or like she would be vulnerable if she opened up about the past to him. Maybe if her mother had still been alive, things would feel different. But even with the house looking the same, too much had changed, what with her father's remarriage. Even Broderick had defected to the Mikkelsons.

Because she remembered very clearly how deeply the Steeles had hated the Mikkelsons. Her dad had labeled them crooks more than once, a strong opinion that had made it easy to accept her adoptive parents' version of the past. That her wealthy and powerful family had corruptive forces all around them, and that someone obviously wanted the Steeles dead. In her mind, Brea had filled in Mikkelson culprits, knowing how fierce that rivalry had been.

But had any of that been true?

Maybe not. But just forgetting all of that enmity and accepting that their rivals were now some kind of family felt unsettling and even a little scary.

There weren't enough breathing exercises in the world to make her okay with any of this. She had to get out of this room for a moment. To regroup.

Brea found herself searching for Ward, needing him at her side.

Six

Stabbing her spoon through her chocolate mousse again and again, Brea was full, done, finished.

And it had more to do with the people than the food.

She was on overload from what should have been a simple meal with her relatives. Coming here had been difficult, but if she didn't step into the lair, she would never have the answers she sought.

Conversation hummed around the table, led mostly by Broderick and Glenna, the others following their lead in pretending this meal was just like any other. She'd hoped having Ward at her side would help, but the meal had still been tense as she sat at the long table the way they'd done in the past. But

things never could be that way again. Finding a path
to a new sense of family was easier said than done.

Aiden's story about the camping trips had left her
even more jittery, with too many memories of those
outings flooding her mind. Many of them focused on
her father, who now sat at the other end of the table.
He didn't pressure her, but she felt his unspoken need
for more from her, for a return to the family fold,
sooner rather than later.

Anxiety churned in her stomach, along with the
king crab and the salad they'd eaten for lunch. She'd
taken note of her childhood-favorite seafood showing up on the menu, and yes, she'd been touched.
How could she forget those earlier memories of her
dad cracking the shells to get the best chunks of
meat for her?

This would be easier if it weren't for the Mikkelsons. Her gaze skipped to Jeannie. The blonde
woman gushed all over Jack, seeming like a happy
newlywed.

Could all of this be real? No hidden agendas? No
culpability from the Mikkelson clan?

Brea's eyes went back to her father, who was cur-
rently holding a sleeping baby in the crook of his
arm, one of Naomi's twin daughters. Brea swallowed
hard. Seeing those two little girls was…tough. Seeing
the way the clan adored them was even tougher, pil-
ing more layers of confusion on her already difficult
past. Seeing all that love she'd missed out on hurt.

Her throat closed up and she abandoned her spoon

"*4 for 4*" MINI-SURVEY

We are prepared to **REWARD** you with 4 FREE books and Free Gifts for completing our MINI SURVEY!

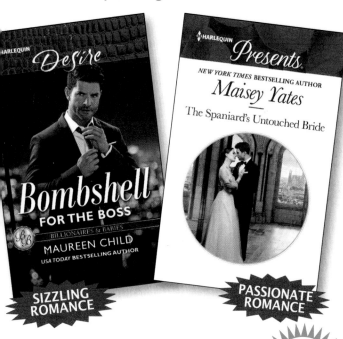

SIZZLING ROMANCE

PASSIONATE ROMANCE

You'll get up to...

4 FREE BOOKS & FREE GIFTS

FREE
Value Over
$20!

just for participating in our Mini Survey!

Get Up To 4 Free Books!

Dear Reader,

IT'S A FACT: if you answer 4 quick questions, we'll send you 4 FREE REWARDS from each series you try!

Try **Harlequin® Desire** books featuring heroes who have it all: wealth, status, incredible good looks...everything but the right woman.

Try **Harlequin Presents® Larger-print** books featuring a sensational and sophisticated world of international romance where sinfully tempting heroes ignite passion.

Or **TRY BOTH!**

I'm not kidding you. As a leading publisher of women's fiction, we value your opinions... and your time. That's why we are prepared to reward you handsomely for completing our mini-survey. In fact, we have 4 Free Rewards for you, including 2 free books and 2 free gifts from each series you try!

Thank you for participating in our survey,

Pam Powers

To get your 4 FREE REWARDS:
Complete the survey below and return the insert today to receive up to 4 FREE BOOKS and FREE GIFTS guaranteed!

"4 for 4" MINI-SURVEY

1 Is reading one of your favorite hobbies?
☐ YES ☐ NO

2 Do you prefer to read instead of watch TV?
☐ YES ☐ NO

3 Do you read newspapers and magazines?
☐ YES ☐ NO

4 Do you enjoy trying new book series with FREE BOOKS?
☐ YES ☐ NO

Please send me my Free Rewards, consisting of **2 Free Books from each series I select** and **Free Mystery Gifts**. I understand that I am under no obligation to buy anything, as explained on the back of this card.

❏ **Harlequin® Desire** (225/326 HDL GNWK)
❏ **Harlequin Presents® Larger-print** (176/376 HDL GNWK)
❏ **Try Both** (225/326/176/376 HDL GNSV)

FIRST NAME   LAST NAME

ADDRESS

APT.#   CITY

STATE/PROV.   ZIP/POSTAL CODE

in the chocolate mousse and angled toward Ward to whisper in his ear, "Gargoyle."

Ward pulled his attention from his conversation with Broderick and nodded quickly. Then looked at his Patek Philippe wristwatch. "This has been great, but I have a conference call I'll need to take at the office." He placed his linen napkin on the table. "Brea and I should be going. I have work to get through."

Broderick inched back his chair. "A meeting on a weekend?"

Standing, Ward shrugged while waiting for Brea. "Just making sure your stockholders are happy."

She couldn't help but see the disappointment in Jack's eyes as she left. Her father always seemed to have such unrealistically high expectations every time their paths crossed. She could understand. And she was trying. She just wished he understood her position, as well. Then maybe she wouldn't feel so smothered.

She'd tried to explain herself to the Steeles in a statement she'd labored over with her lawyer. Doing her best to fill in the gaps for them with a summary of what had happened with her other family after they rescued her from the crash site. Brea had hoped the Steeles would see how tangled the truth of her reality had become. But what had felt like an outpouring of emotion on her end had apparently come across as terse and aloof on the other.

Another curse from her years away.

She wasn't on the same emotional or mental footing as these people.

To his credit, Ward had made good on their safe word. He whisked her quickly and convincingly away toward the coatrack, which was flanked by family photographs on the wall.

Brea averted her eyes, feeling for her thick blue parka. Sliding into her coat, she smiled at Ward. The sound of her family's laughter and conversation hung in the air as he passed her a wool scarf.

Just like that, the walls of her childhood home seemed to close in on her. Ward spoke in hushed tones to a staff member about getting his SUV brought around. She pushed past him, stepping across the threshold into the crisp night air.

An involuntary shiver pulsed through her spine in the frigid air. And yet the physical sensation was welcomed. As was the smell of pine and cold. Familiar smells. Yes. But smells not completely tied to her past here.

The past she couldn't quite make sense of as hard as she tried.

Behind her, she heard the door clicking open to reveal Ward. Warm light from inside washed over his black wool jacket. He yanked on a hat, shading his blue eyes from the sun, which was already sinking at midday.

Royce shouldered through the door before it closed, flipping up the lapel of his long wool coat as he stopped beside them, his gaze locked on Brea. "Do you have a minute to talk?"

"Sure," she said, nervous and curious all at once about what her twin's husband had to say away from the others.

As anxious as she'd been to depart and leave behind the pressure of all the family together, Brea didn't have that same level of nervousness now. Speaking to Royce one-on-one—speaking to any of them one-on-one—was always easier for her. Fewer agendas to sift through. Less noise for her brain.

Royce bristled as a wave of wind tumbled through the Steele compound. His eyes were soft in the yellow-orange hues of the sky. "The Steeles are a great family. But I understand how overwhelming they can be in full force," he said with insight. "Naomi and I are heading to North Dakota to check out the pipeline construction." Royce was a research scientist, who was responsible for groundbreaking ecological innovations in the oil industry. "Chuck Mikkelson's in charge of that arm of the operation, but you and Ward could both join us. You can still call it work, but it would also give you two some time away from feeling obligated to come to these family meals."

For a quiet guy, he sure noticed a lot. Still, as much as she wanted to figure out what happened, she balked at the thought of going to stay on a Mikkelson's home turf.

Her stomach twisted at the idea of spending time

with any of the Mikkelsons. With her vision turning fuzzy, she took a settling breath. Focused her eyes on the tree line, where a few elk weaved around low-hanging limbs.

"Chuck's wife has struggled with amnesia," Royce reminded them, his breath visible in the cold air. "She may also have some insights when it comes to reconciling all the mixed-up parts of your past."

Brea chewed her bottom lip. "She might." Her chest went tight with anxiety. Maybe Shana Mikkelson would understand this anxiety, too. "It's generous of you to mention this opportunity and invite us on your trip."

The scientist arched an eyebrow. "I'm not totally altruistic with this. My wife wants time with her twin. I want that for her—peace, reconciliation. I'm not good at romantic gestures, but this trip falling over Valentine's Day would make it a perfect gift for her."

Her heart hammered as Brea inhaled a deep breath of cold air. It stung in her lungs as night birds squawked in the towering pines.

Valentine's Day? She hadn't even given a thought to the impending "lover's holiday." Her skin prickled, and it had nothing to do with the cold and everything to do with her sexy lover as Ward placed a steadying hand on her back. "How long were you planning to stay?"

Brea shifted on her feet, sleet crunching beneath her sheepskin-lined leather boots. Filled with the urgency to run, she imagined what it would be like to dash headlong for the elk loping in the tree line. To leave all of this behind.

"It'll be a three-day, two-night trip." Royce leveled a stare at Brea. "You need to understand. I'd do anything for her—and anything to protect her."

Maybe she should have taken that as the warning it was no doubt meant to be. But Brea couldn't deny a certain satisfaction that Naomi had found someone to stand beside her.

Ward might not have shared her feelings about Royce's warning, however. She felt tension in the arm he slung more tightly around her shoulders.

"I'm sure you understand, I feel the same." Ward held the other man's gaze for a moment to let that sink in. "It's time for us to leave."

As they strode toward the SUV, she thought about how easy it was to lean into the strength of Ward's protective arm, to pretend their fake relationship was in fact becoming something more than a one-month agreement.

But she also recalled his grief over his broken marriage and losing his stepdaughter. The memory of the pain in his voice when he'd shared that still tore right through her, speaking to a part of her that understood what it was like to lose everything.

Sleeping together had been incredible, but it put them in a dangerous position on so many levels. Emotionally and practically. What would come of their affair if she found that the Mikkelsons—or the

Steeles—had played a role in that crash? She wasn't sure, but she guessed where Ward's loyalties would lie. He'd worked too hard for this position to turn his back on the Steeles.

Beyond that, she wasn't even sure she could trust her memories, her past or her family. How could she pursue something real and long-term with him when she was still getting to know herself?

And where would that leave her? She wanted to think she could simply walk away. But the more time she spent with him, the more difficult she realized that would be. So before they celebrated any kind of Valentine's Day together—before she slid back into his bed again—she needed to figure out a plan B, for when things fell apart.

Because she wasn't sure she could handle her world falling apart again, especially when she still wasn't over everything that had happened to her.

Pressing his foot down on the accelerator, Ward maneuvered his SUV through the massive, elaborate gates that enclosed the Steele compound.

"What do you think about making that trip to North Dakota? We don't have to go if you prefer not to."

To block the sinking sun, he flicked the visor down, more eager for her answer than he should be—eager to spend time alone with her away from the larger contingent of her family. He'd been playing the role of buffer. Her family was one of the reasons they'd started.

He waited for her answer as he drove toward the setting sun. Short Alaskan winter days sent the sun's rays shrinking behind the mountains all the way back to Brea's apartment.

"It sounds like I could learn a lot about the newly merged family business."

He mulled over her words. Was she already thinking about ways to play sleuth on Mikkelson territory, as she'd likely done around Ward's office the day that had launched this dating charade? What would Brea's family think if they knew about the information he suspected she'd taken off Ward's computer? He was risking his job by not telling anyone. But once he'd figured out what records she'd accessed, he'd determined there was nothing proprietary involved and decided to keep the incident to himself.

Glancing to his right, he watched the way silence made her mouth grow taut. He hated seeing her uneasy.

Clearing his throat, he turned onto the main road. "And it really doesn't bother you that Naomi and Royce are the ones who invited us? That Marshall Steele is going to be our pilot?"

She twisted her hands in her lap, picking at her fingernails. "I can't avoid my siblings forever just because I'm afraid the world will open up under me if I gain total clarity about my past."

"Is that really how you feel?" He held her gaze for a moment. "We don't have to go."

"I'm not afraid." She tipped her chin, eyes full of that fiery determination he admired.

Once he had stopped at a red light, he reached over to stroke her jaw briefly before returning to the steering wheel. "It's going to be a quick trip, but it also sounds like a good idea. Like Royce said, you could get a breather from so many people here, while still getting to know the Steeles—and Mikkelsons— in smaller groups."

Brea toyed with her hair, rubbing it between her fingers. "What if I change my mind? You could go without me."

What was she hedging about? He understood the lunch had been stressful, but throughout the meal, she'd leaned on him, touched his knee under the table. Something had shifted when they were outside, and he wasn't sure what that might be.

He accelerated again into traffic, sludge crunching under the tires. "For the business, I should go. But if we're apart over Valentine's Day, it sounds like you're not holding up your end of our bargain. People will question why we're not together."

"Well, we can't have people gossiping." Brea's jaw tightened as she reached to hold her hands in front of the heater vents. The scent of her perfume drifted toward him on the gusts of warm air.

Ward drew in a deep breath, then looked at her, her face so beautiful, bathed in the warm glow of the dashboard lights. "I want to spend time with you."

Flicking the blinker on, he turned onto a road where a light dusting of snow had begun to accumulate.

Turning her head to face the window, she muttered, "Spend time in my bed, you mean."

He detected something dark in her voice. Careening his head to see her, he noticed the way she chewed her bottom lip.

"Is that a problem?"

The red light just ahead of them turned green. An ancient snowplow lurched forward in a sputter of black smoke. Ward steered the SUV around the choking vehicle.

The leather creaked as Brea shifted in the seat. "I just want to be sure we're on the same page about what's happening between us. This is an arrangement that allows me to be around my family with your protection. And I'm helping you blend into the family corporate culture."

"And the sex?"

The question hung in the air in between them. Electricity palpable before she answered. "The sex was amazing, truly amazing. But it can't be anything more."

He agreed, but hearing her say as much still stung. "I don't recall saying otherwise."

She looked down at her hands, her hair rippling in front of her eyes like a curtain. "The family vacation to North Dakota just seems…like something more."

"It's not a vacation. It's business."

"And our timeline to break up is still the same?"

Was that regret in her voice?

He pulled off the road, into a parking lot, and turned to face her. "If that's what you want. I thought I made it clear I'm not interested in a white picket fence. Been there. Done that. Have the battle scars to prove it." He stroked her hair back over her shoulder, lingering to caress her neck. "But that doesn't change how much I want you. And after what we experienced, I'm not backing off."

He sealed his vow with a kiss. He intended it to be a brief skim of his lips over hers. But she gripped his jacket and pulled him closer, sighing. The kiss quickly spun out of control. But then Ward had learned things were often that way with Brea. Never had he met a woman who turned him on as fully and as quickly as she did.

She was a feast for the senses. The hint of her floral shampoo, the taste of chocolate mousse she'd picked at. Best of all, the satin texture of her skin. He wanted to take her here, now—

A car door slammed near them, a few parking spots away, and they bolted apart. His heartbeat sped up, heat still flaring up the back of his shoulders from wanting her. Damn, he'd lost sight of where they were. She deserved better from him.

"Your place or mine?" he asked, hunger for her edging his words with stark need.

"I'm—" She hesitated. Licked her lips. "I'm not sure that's a good idea."

Surprise—and a hefty dose of disappointment—

rushed through him. Especially since he could see her pulse jumping in the fast-ticking vein in her neck, where he'd just kissed her. "Why not?"

"I don't regret what we did." She stroked his face lightly, as if unable to trust herself to deepen the connection. "But things are moving too fast for me. I need space to think."

He saw the resolution in her deep brown eyes and knew enough about negotiations to realize he wasn't going to win this round. "You're right, of course. This afternoon had to be rough for you."

A hint of regret chased that resolution in her gaze. "I wonder what it would have been like if we'd met each other on totally neutral territory."

He wondered the same. But they would never know. He could only go with the hand they'd been dealt, and his resolve to keep her close was strong as ever. He needed to keep her in his sights. Yes, this was about helping him gain entry to the family, and being her buffer. But it was also about making sure she was on the up-and-up.

And if he wanted to return to those out-of-control kisses and the passion that swept them both away, he damned well intended to make sure she had an unforgettable Valentine's Day.

The past two days preparing for the trip to North Dakota, Brea found her mind full of Ward. Thoughts of what it would be like if she hadn't turned him away.

She was more apprehensive about seeing Chuck

Mikkelson than she'd expected. While he was too young to have had anything to do with the crash, if his family was involved, she feared his reaction when the truth came out.

If only she could trust Ward with all her concerns. She felt so alone.

Which was a feeling exacerbated as she sat white-knuckled in the small private airplane. Marshall, her brother, acted as pilot. Flying them over the impossibly blue lakes in Canada.

Inching toward the window, Brea made herself look out. Her stomach promptly plummeted as her gaze rested on a snowcapped mountain. Painful shards of her past rose to her consciousness, as intently as the peaks below her did.

This flight to North Dakota stirred memories in her. Not just from the crash, which she'd expected. But of that life before. The life after. Life with her adoptive parents and the things they'd done as a family and with their tight-knit community.

She'd spent so much time recovering from the crash and her mother's death, dazed and full of grief. By the time she'd healed in the home of Steven and Karen Jones, she'd stopped questioning why her father hadn't come for her. She'd believed Jack Steele had given up on her. That the Steeles and their circles were corrupt. And she'd been so empty inside, needing a family to fill the void. She'd gladly accepted the Joneses' invitation to stay, to be their daughter. Life was simpler in their home. Sparse. Orderly. Emotions were more predictable. Restrained. All of that had appealed to her when she'd been hurting so badly inside, she thought she might fly apart at any moment.

The twin engines of the private jet hummed. Became something like white noise as she released her grip from the leather seat below her. Looking at the shimmering lakes beneath the plane, she found herself thinking about her off-the-grid upbringing. Or should she say second upbringing?

Steven Jones had been the community's electrician, working with micro hydro and wind sources for energy to power the small group of homes. He'd taken her along when she was maybe fourteen years old, once she'd realized she wouldn't be leaving. No one was coming for her. She'd been eager to belong. Confused, but desperate to keep her place in the world she'd found herself in. She'd soaked up the way he assessed different weak points in the systems, gladly throwing herself into a completely new world.

Swallowing a lump in her throat, she cast a look to Marshall. Rather than sitting in the back, she'd opted to sit close to her brother, in the cockpit. Family bonding. Her brother wore the headset, his thick dark curls in need of a cut.

Though maybe next time she ought to choose a less-traumatic space as grounds for her healing with her estranged family. With as much time as she'd spent in counseling about her past, she ought to have known better than to throw herself headlong into difficult situations.

It was almost painful sitting there, with her anxiety about flights and her family keeping her on edge. But after their last conversation, she wasn't comfortable sitting by Ward.

In the back of the cabin, he clacked away on his laptop. Keystrokes muffled by the sound of the engine. But as she glanced over her shoulder, she noticed the way he threw himself into work. Brow furrowed. A pencil tucked behind his ear.

Her twin also busied herself with work. A flurry of papers surrounded her. Naomi's lips pursed as she made her way through a brief. Royce was sleeping. Life with twins had clearly drained him. The girls had stayed back with Jack and Jeannie, as well as Delaney, who was on hand to assist during the short trip away.

Swiveling in her seat, Brea forced her attention back to Marshall, whose steady gaze kept the plane even. For a moment she felt as though some of the air returned to her lungs. Impossibly, she felt a surge of trust in her brother's ability to deliver them safely. He'd always been a quiet kid in their noisy family, but whatever Marshall had tackled, he'd done well. He paid attention to detail, and it showed. They'd all seen that from him at a young age.

"Thank you for flying us today, Marshall."

"No problem," he said. "It's a good opportunity to log some flight hours. I'm also going to take in a rodeo while I'm there before resting up for our flight back."

She wasn't surprised he didn't plan to join them at the pipeline site. He'd always been more of a loner than the others in their family.

"I'm surprised you enjoy flying," she ventured. "You didn't like it when we were kids. And then with the crash…" She hesitated. "Or maybe I'm remembering wrong about when we were kids. Was it Broderick who was nervous about planes?"

He shook his head, an easy smile on his lips. "No, it was me. After you and Mom were in the crash, I decided I had to conquer the fear. Maybe it sounds strange. But I felt like if I conquered the sky somehow, it would be a way of paying tribute to you both."

Brea's throat closed with emotion. No matter what else she might believe about her Steele siblings, their love for their mother was without question. Would it have helped her get past her own fierce sense of loss if she could have grieved with them?

She swallowed hard and said, "Tell me something about our past."

He glanced at her. "Are you sure that's a good idea? I wouldn't want to do anything to mess with your therapy." He hesitated. "Especially when we're in the air. I can tell this isn't easy for you, Brea."

Touched, she felt the warmth of gratitude for his keen observation.

"Delaney and Aiden shared some things with me, and it helped." In fact, after listening, she found it easier to trust them. "Please, pick something…"

Her pleading eyes met his. He nodded, under-

standing drawing tension away from his jaw and brow
before he returned his attention to the windscreen.

"Sure," he said somberly. "Remember that day
we flew together, and Dad let me take the yoke…"

*Marshall had always been closer to Brea than to
Naomi, and sometimes he felt left out, since the two
of them were thick as thieves. His grandma said it
was the twin bond. That didn't make him feel any
better.*

*Naomi was supposed to go on the flight today,
but she'd canceled at the last minute to go fishing
with their grandmother. So Marshall had jumped at
the chance to spend time with Brea without having
to compete with her twin. Even though he hated flying. The sensation of looking down at the ground.
He nervously tightened his seat belt.*

*Brea sat next to him. Understood his unease. She
tightened her high ponytail, her attention turning to
her father, who smiled behind aviator glasses.*

*Pointing excitedly, Brea squealed. "Wow, that's
our house. And the boathouse. And the horses are so
tiny. This is so cool. Can I hold the steering wheel?"*

*"It's called a yoke," Jack Steele said patiently.
Beaming at the interest his children were taking in
the flight.*

*"The yoke." Brea squinted her eyes, inquisitive
as ever. "Can I touch the one on this side?"*

"As long as you let me know before you touch it."

"Okay," she said, her ponytail bobbing like crazy, she nodded so fast. "I'm letting you know."

Their dad laughed. "That's my fearless girl."

"That's Naomi."

"You too, kiddo."

Marshall felt like a coward. So he said, "Dad, I wanna fly."

With shaking hands, Marshall approached the yoke. He grasped on to it with all the gusto of a World-War-II-era fighter pilot.

Made himself look out to the horizon, the colors whooshing before him. His stomach as choppy as an uneasy sea. And that sea rose within him until he felt the burning sensation of vomit bubble in the back of his throat.

No. No. No. Not like this. He could tamp it down. Had to.

But then there was the expanse of land before him. The height. And try as he might, he could not stop the hiccup of vomit from exploding out of his mouth and down the caribou shirt his grandmother had given him.

Cheeks burning, he fled to the small on-plane bathroom to wipe his mouth.

Brea was there, waiting for him when he left the bathroom. She knelt beside him, passing him a wash-cloth like their mom would have done. "Marshall, you're good on horses. I'm scared of falling off."

He knew she meant well, but it didn't help him feel any better. Steeles didn't flinch. They didn't give up. Ever...

* * *

With her brother's words still echoing in her mind, Brea stared out the aircraft window, the North Dakota plains stretching out for miles and miles. Far away from Alaska, leaving even Canada behind.

Maybe this trip was a good idea after all. Time away from both parts of her childhood, and a chance to embrace tomorrow rather than the past.

Because thinking about any part of her childhood knocked her more and more off-balance at a time when she needed to keep her head straight. If any one of the Mikkelsons was involved in trying to harm her family, she couldn't afford to let her guard down.

This time with Chuck Mikkelson could offer a chance to ferret out clues about the day her world imploded, breaking her ties with everyone who'd once been so important to her.

Seven

Ward had been to forty-two states over the course of his career, but this was his first trip to North Dakota. And normally he would have been all about the job, about the new insights on the pipeline. Not today. He just wanted to finish the meeting and get Brea alone, to see if he could persuade her to reclaim the explosive chemistry they'd shared too briefly.

He forced his attention back on work for the moment, since the faster he finished here, the sooner he could return with her to their hotel suite. At least maybe he could get more hints about what made her tick. He stomped his boots to get the circulation flowing again in his feet as they stood in the frigid weather. Snow whipped all around this section of

the pipeline. He was used to cold, having lived in
Alaska, but the wind sweeping across the Dakota
plains had a bite that stole his breath.

But despite the bone-cold scrape of the wind,
Shana and Chuck Mikkelson seemed to love their
new home state.

Ward stayed back a step, listening as Chuck gave
them all a tour of the modifications on the pipeline. He covered everything from innovations made,
thanks to Royce's work on efficiency, to the safety
upgrades.

Lord, this was a stark wasteland. They'd traveled
for two hours in a luxury RV. Chuck said he'd bought
the vehicle because of how often they traveled out to
remote sites. If they were caught in a storm, he and
Shana could park the RV and ride out the weather in
their own little home away from home. There was
even a storage compartment underneath for a car if
they needed to park at a work site and wanted the
freedom of a smaller vehicle.

Wind whistling past his ears, Ward wondered what
Brea was making of all of this. Was she glad she'd
come? Or was she feeling stressed? She had stayed
glued to his side, and he wasn't sure if that was to
play along with their fake relationship or because she
genuinely needed him. She'd made a point of wanting to be here, but had stayed unusually quiet since
they'd arrived, especially once Marshall had headed
off to catch a rodeo on his own.

It seemed to him she was avoiding Naomi. Which

was hard to do in these luxurious, yet close, quarters. But he couldn't determine why.

Snow came down faster, the wind blowing it sideways. Hard. Pellets stung his cheeks.

Chuck angled a look at Ward while tugging his overcoat collar up more securely over his ears. "Should we put this tour on hold due to weather?"

Ward cocked an eyebrow. "I doubt it's going to get much better for a couple of months. So I'd just as soon we finish today. Royce? Your thoughts?"

"Press on," the man of few words replied.

Her blond hair peeking free from her hood, Shana Mikkelson waved a gloved hand toward Naomi and Brea. "Let's get some coffee in the RV."

Indecision chased across Brea's wind-reddened features. She bit her chapped lip and then said, "Sure, I could use something warm."

So much for getting clues about her by watching Brea with her sister. He studied Brea's retreating figure as she left his side, her thick braid specked with ice and snow.

Chuck adjusted his Stetson, pulling it further down his head, covering more of his golden-brown hair. "I'm glad you could both make it here. There's a lot of work left to be done, but it's an exciting new venture for the company."

Ward forced his thoughts back to the job at hand, focusing on Chuck and the work he was doing here. Networking was an underrated portion of the CEO job, but something that always paid off. "How's your move coming with starting the new job?"

Shrugging against the wind, Chuck angled his body toward Ward and Royce. Snow began to accumulate on his wool coat. "We're building a place on a ten-acre piece of land that already had a converted barn on the property. It's great to be on-site and watch every stage of the process. We figure the barn will make a great guesthouse, too."

Royce stuffed his hands into his coat pockets. "Looking forward to seeing it."

"You're staying with us, of course," Chuck said, his voice rising to combat the wind.

Sharing an afternoon together was one thing. Staying under the same roof was another, and an arrangement Ward didn't think Brea would want. "I made reservations downtown."

"We have plenty of space at the house," Chuck offered. "Guest rooms and a loft."

Ward whistled. "That must be a mighty big barn. I'll see what Brea thinks."

Chuck nodded. "Family is important to us. Leaving Alaska was a big transition, one we felt we needed to make for our marriage. But we want to maintain the close relationships we have, especially once we have kids. Hopefully the house will be done before the baby needs a nursery."

"You're expecting?" Ward extended his hand, trying not to think of the stepdaughter he couldn't see. "Congratulations."

"We're adopting." Chuck shook his hand, a smile of pure happiness spreading across his face. "The timing could be tomorrow, or months, or years from now. We have to wait until they match us to a child. We're just glad to be together after a rough patch not too long ago."

"Good to hear it."

Chuck's eyes narrowed as he squinted against the pelting snowfall. "If you don't mind my asking, how did you and Brea become an item?"

"We met through the business. Alaska Oil Barons, Inc., sure does host more than its fair share of charity events, and Brea and I ended up in the same corners of the room a few times. She's a beautiful woman," Ward said simply, honestly. Best to keep it straight-forward. Private.

"I'm just surprised she'll have anything to do with the company after all her reservations about coming back into the family fold."

Ward didn't intend to tell him that she wasn't fully embracing the family—not yet. "She was gone for a long time."

Kicking the snow beneath his boot, Ward noticed the way stress lines creased the corners of Chuck's mouth. "She seems to resent us, the Mikkelsons. How she could blame my mom—or even Jack—is beyond me. I've found no proof that anyone in the business had anything to do with that crash. I've searched my father's records at length."

"And Brea knows this?" Ward couldn't keep the surprise out of his voice.

"I've told my mother. A lot of rumors floated around at the time of the accident, especially because of the deep rivalry between the families." Chuck shook his head. "But there's just no proof my family had anything to do with it."

Royce, who had been content to observe the conversation, cleared his throat. His quiet sensibility was something Ward appreciated. The man didn't waste words. He had a scientist's way of synthesizing important elements.

"It can be very difficult to accept that sometimes accidents just happen."

Chuck thumped a piece of equipment. "I'm obviously relieved Brea's alive. But it's tough watching this family feel all torn up again, between the merger and the riding accident Jack had last year…"

"And your mother's marriage…" Ward reminded him.

The family had gone through a lot in a short period of time. He felt for them, but Brea was his priority.

"Yeah," Chuck agreed, sighing out a white cloud into the cold air, "that was a shocker."

It didn't appear Chuck Mikkelson had any new insights to offer, as much as Ward would have wished otherwise, for Brea's sake. "Let's finish up out here before we freeze our asses off."

Both men agreed, and Chuck launched back into

details on the gauges and valves, waving for them to follow him to a garage-sized workshop full of control panels.

Anticipation charged through Ward. He was that much closer to ending the workday. That only left an obligatory supper out, and then he could move forward with plans to get Brea alone at the hotel.

He only wished he had better news to share with her about her search for answers. Because, truth be told, he guessed that her personal quest was the main reason she'd taken this trip.

And her being here didn't really have a damned thing to do with him.

He shouldn't be bothered by her reaction. He wasn't in the market for a serious relationship after being burned by his ex. Paisley had paid the biggest price, and that hurt him most.

After such a massive mistake, he was better off focusing on what he did best, running the Alaska Oil Barons, Inc.

Brea looked around the RV that was as large as some of the off-the-grid houses in her former community. And definitely far more luxurious with a buttery-soft leather wrap-around sofa and a recliner. Decorated in warm browns, tans and copper, the space made for a lovely home away from home.

Shana stood at the counter, making coffee, while Naomi sat crossed-legged on the couch. It was so surreal being in the same space with her twin after so many years apart. They'd been so close once. Would they ever be so again?

The other two women's conversation hummed around Brea, and she turned her attention to stare out the window at Ward, his shoulders broad, taller than the other men who wore Stetsons.

"Don't you agree, Brea?"

She looked back quickly at her twin. "I'm sorry. What did you say?"

Naomi tapped the window pane, gesturing toward the men outside, whom Brea had been staring at. "Royce has made brilliant innovations for a cleaner transfer of oil."

"Oh, yes, it's fascinating on a number of levels." Brea couldn't help but be intrigued personally, too. "In my community, getting those sorts of cutting-edge inventions was often difficult, due to being so separate from the rest of the world."

Maybe if the village had been more accessible, she would have been found? That shift in her thinking gave her pause.

Shana's hand moved with smooth efficiency as she pulled mugs from the cabinet. "I'm glad we had a quiet day to look over things. Chuck's brother got caught in the middle of quite a scene with the media last summer."

Brea had read up on the Mikkelsons and the younger son, Trystan, who had been in scrapes with the press. "He's the one who married his media consultant."

"They have a baby boy," Shana said wistfully, then smiled as the coffee maker gurgled. "We're planning to adopt. It's going to happen for us, I just get impatient."

Brea hadn't given much thought to having children. Since her teenage years, her life had been so consumed with figuring out the past and how to weave whatever she found into her present so she could move forward with the future. But right now, she found her thoughts captivated by the notion of holding an infant in her arms.

What an unsettling notion, though, the idea of permanence, family, longevity—especially when she could barely wrap her brain around the notion of an affair.

The aroma of hazelnut and coffee beans filled the luxury RV.

Brea's gaze slid to the window overlooking the trio of men striding across the icy lot, toward a large garage-like area. Ward was so tall and imposing, his long-legged steps confident and sure-footed. Could she really hold strong to her decision not to sleep with him again? She wanted to give in to temptation, but the strength of that draw made her all the more cautious. She needed to tread warily for just that reason. Their simple affair wasn't turning out to be so simple after all.

Shana set a bamboo tray of stoneware coffee mugs down on the small table in front of Brea. Steam rolled from the mugs, and both twins blew over their steaming cup of java at the same time.

Brea looked up self-consciously. An echo of her grandmother's words whispered through her.

It's the twin bond.

Shana had already made her way back to the coffeepot and was filling a silver thermos. "I'm going to take some coffee out to the guys." She waved them back to their seats. "Don't get up. I can carry it all."

Thermos under her arm, she carried stacked cups and opened the door. A blast of frigid air filled with snow rolled inside. The door closed after her, slamming from the force of the wind.

Naomi looked at her sister. "I know this whole situation is awkward, but I don't want you to feel uncomfortable around me as we figure out how to be a family again."

"Thank you." Brea poured creamer into her coffee. "And I'm trying to push past the awkwardness. It's just scary to me that there are still a lot of unanswered questions about what happened. You should be worried too, for your girls."

She glanced up at the array of Mikkelson family photographs on the built-in bookcase. Her eyes focused on one of the older photographs of the Mikkelson clan as she remembered them from her limited exposure in the past—this was the family who had been their bitter business rivals.

Her stomach catapulted at the image.

Naomi shivered, her arms wrapping protectively

around herself. "You can't really believe someone is still out to get us."

Her twin's eyes were concerned, but not suspicious. Not accusing. Whatever Naomi might believe, she was at least inclined to listen with an open mind, and Brea appreciated that. So often since she'd returned, she felt like she had to weigh every word.

"I think someone could have a reason to hide what they did. You're a lawyer. You should know that."

Naomi bit her bottom lip. "Okay, I can see your point. Whatever you need me to do help you investigate, I want you to know, I'm on board. I'm sure Shana would offer her professional assistance, too. She's a top-notch investigator."

"I know. She found me." Brea's skin prickled. "If it's okay, I'd rather refrain from involving the Mikkelsons any more than we have to."

"So, you really think they…" Naomi's words hung in the air between them as the aggressive wind rocked the RV slightly.

"I think their loyalty to each other could make them close their eyes to possibilities and make it tougher for me to find the truth. What if it were Charles Mikkelson Sr.? How far would they go to protect his memory?"

Brea looked away from her twin's horrified expression, the pinch of guilt over inflicting pain on the family making Brea uncomfortable. She peered outside, watching Shana pass the thermos and cups to the men inside the shelter of the open garage that was big as a hangar.

"But if it was him, he's dead now and not a threat," Naomi pointed out logically.

Naomi leaned forward, putting her mug of coffee down on the side table.

Brea considered her twin's words, her attention wandering around the luxury RV. Little touches of photographs and Alaska memorabilia—knickknacks, such as elk and bear figurines, on the shelves—showed the blended life of Shana and Chuck. Normally, personal touches would be comforting.

But in this situation?

She couldn't shake the feeling that there was more to the Mikkelsons—something she was missing. Some sign of foul play in relation to the plane crash. And while she didn't want to believe it could be these people she now had to call family…

"Or there could have been others involved, along with him." Her eyes went out of focus for a second, lingering back on the pictures on the bookshelf. "Once I know the truth, I hope the path forward will be simple for us all."

"As do I." Naomi uncrossed her legs, leather creaking with the movement.

Brea tried to put together the right thing to say, and found there were no perfect words for something like this. She drew in a deep inhale of coffee and leather. She squeezed her eyes shut, resolved to talk, knowing the time frame would never be right. "How will Dad feel if Jeannie's family is involved? Will he even believe the truth? Or will he subconsciously block me from finding out a truth he can't bear to know? I honestly don't want to see him hurt."

Slowly, Naomi nodded. "I can understand that."

A keening bark of North Dakota wind added its lonely wail to their dark conversation.

"Really?" Brea hadn't expected that concession. "Thank you. It makes it easier to talk to you if there aren't expectations in place that I can't meet."

Pushing her lips into a sad kind of smile, Naomi gathered her dark hair into a ponytail, changing the waterfall effect it had while cascading onto her cashmere sweater. "In the interest of honesty, the counselor the family and I have been talking with made it clear that expectation management is important."

"The family counselor," Brea repeated, making sure she understood that correctly. "You're *all* seeing a therapist?" She blinked, surprise circulating through her.

"Felicity suggested it, and we all agreed it was a good idea. We want what's best for you. And…" Naomi paused to swallow heavily, the mug of coffee untouched in her hand. "Dad's been struggling with renewed grief over Mom. We all want to be there for him."

Her sister's shoulders slumped. It might have been a long time since they'd lived together as sisters, but Brea could still read the hurt and pain in Naomi's eyes. Brea stood up on shaky legs. Willed them to move across the small distance to her sister. Settling onto the leather couch next to Naomi, Brea gulped down air.

"She's been gone so long." Brea twisted her hands in her lap.

"But you still miss her too, right?"

Brea looked up sharply, hoping the answer was already plain in her eyes. "Of course." Their mother had died in fear for Brea, holding her in her arms until Brea blacked out, surrounding her with a mother's love. That loss had been the toughest of all those Brea had sustained. "It couldn't have been easy for you, losing Mom, then you getting cancer."

It really hit her then that her sister could have died. That she could have missed the opportunity to see Naomi again. Her throat clogged. Why hadn't the twin connection worked to alert her? Brea pressed two fingers to a headache that was suddenly blooming.

"It was a difficult time after you were gone. I missed Mom. I missed you. I missed my hair," Naomi said with a wry grin that slowly faded. "And I was terrified of what it would do to Dad if he lost me, too."

A sharp pain pierced Brea's chest. Her twin's pain.

"I wish I could have been there for you." Brea touched her sister's hand lightly.

"Thank you." Naomi clasped Brea's hand tightly. "I have my husband and my twins. And now I have my sister back… At least I hope I do."

"I'm trying," Brea admitted, although she felt twitchy and wanted to pull her hand back. Instead she carefully eased it away. The quick flash of disappointment on Naomi's face made Brea feel petty and small.

"Well," Naomi said in a lowered voice, "remember when we sisters all wanted to be mermaids, and I made us stay at the pool, working on our synchronized mermaid dives until our fingers wrinkled from being in the water so long?"

Brea laughed, her smile lighting up her face. "I do. And after our swims, Mom would braid our hair while it was still wet so we would have waves the next day."

A memory chased through Brea's mind, one of those that she couldn't quite tell if it was real or something she'd just dreamed in those first months at the Joneses' house. "Did she braid our hair for—" she searched for a way to ask the question while still leaving part of it unsaid, to see if Naomi's story matched Brea's recollection "—special events?"

"Yes," Naomi said excitedly. "Mom loved going to *The Nutcracker* at Christmas. She would always braid our hair prior, and then put matching red plaid bows in yours and mine."

Her words matched what was in Brea's mind so perfectly, down to the bows. "Could you tell me more?"

"I would like that," Naomi answered without hesitation. "The Christmas before your accident, we'd both decided we were too old for braids, but Delaney wanted them, and Dad told us to make her and Mom happy…"

Naomi huffed with an angry sigh, crossing her arms over her chest stubbornly. She wasn't giving in without a fight. "I don't want go to a play. I want to go sledding."

Their mother nodded, though Mary pointed for Brea to sit, a vintage brush in her hands. "We'll do that, too. Tomorrow."

Sledding sounded more fun than a play they'd already seen every year of their lives. She was getting too old for kid stuff. She just had to convince her mom, although it would be nice if her sisters would chime in and help.

"We should skip the ballet and go to bed early so we won't be tired."

Mom didn't miss a beat brushing through Brea's hair, working out the tangles before starting the French braid. "We could skip sledding altogether if it's too tiring for you."

"Fine," Naomi sighed, wishing Brea would have helped her fight the battle. "I'll get ready for the ballet."

"This is about making memories," Mom said, crossing clusters of hair, one over the other. "Someday you'll all be grown-up, and you'll do this with your kids."

Delaney looked up from her book in the corner of

the room. Her braids were already completed and tied with a bow. These braids were special, Mom had told them. She'd been taught by her Native Alaskan grandmother. Part of keeping the tribal traditions alive, even as Alaska modernized.

Closing her book, Delaney asked, "But there are so many of us. When we grow up, how will you and Dad be able to pick which one of our houses to go to?"

Brea looked at her reflection in a handheld mirror. "Mom could come to one. Dad could go to another. And Delaney will get Uncle Conrad."

Delaney's bottom lip trembled, and a tear rolled down her cheek.

Mom gently cooed, still brushing Brea's hair. "We'll fly everyone home, and we'll all go to the ballet together."

But Naomi's brows furrowed. All together? Something seemed off in that statement.

She imagined traveling faraway sometimes, where no one could find her while she wrote a book and became a famous author. You had to be a hermit to be an author. That's what her favorite television character had said, and she seemed glamorous enough for anything she said to be true.

Mom's fingers moved quickly, expertly. "How about I tell the story you always ask your grandmother to tell at bedtime? You always say it gets better each time. Maybe The Nutcracker *could be like that."*

Naomi knew when she was beaten. And truth be told, she liked the story. "Okay, since we've got time to kill while you finish our hair. Tell us 'The Legend of...'"

Brea soaked in her sister's words, finding that each one opened a doorway to her memories that matched perfectly. So poignant. And sad.

They'd been so unaware of the pain ahead of them.

She wished she'd paid more attention to the moment, enjoyed the feel of her mother brushing her hair. Or the oral tradition her mother instilled in them. The stories of her mother's tribe. The way she'd wake them with songs.

Brea hadn't thought about that time in years. How much else had she lost of her childhood? She wanted to remember. She tried...but she couldn't quite grab it; the memories too elusive.

Something that chilled her until she realized the men had returned and the door was open.

Her gaze collided with Ward's.

Ice flecked his hair and brows, making him look like some elemental prince of winter come home at last. His wind-chapped, chiseled face was somehow made more handsome from the environment. It brought out the deep blue of his eyes. Awareness tingled over her in the way she was beginning to learn was standard around this man.

"Everything okay?" His question was clearly only directed at her.

But rather than making Brea feel weak or pressured, she felt…protected. And not in a smothering way. He looked like he cared, but he hadn't swept her out of the room.

"I'm fine, thank you." She smiled at him. "We're sharing childhood stories. I'm remembering things. It's okay."

The truth of that simple statement warmed her inside, while his hand on her shoulder stirred a different kind of heat.

Remembering a sweetness in her past that she'd forgotten made her want to celebrate this momentary pocket of joy and peace in the most elemental way. She knew too well the pain of loss, how quickly life could change for the worse. Spurred by her memories and the loss of her mother, all her reasons for not sleeping with him seemed to evaporate.

Wise or not, she knew when they got back to their hotel room, she and Ward would be sharing a bed.

Shaking the ice off his coat, Ward's hand went to the back of his neck as he took in the surprise of seeing Brea and Naomi sitting close to each other.

"Sorry to have interrupted," he said.

Brea's eyes danced. "Naomi was going to tell me 'The Legend of Qalupalik.' It was a favorite for most of us when we were kids, but it's been so long since I heard it…" She bit her bottom lip for a moment before continuing, "I'm not sure I remember it correctly."

Ward waved toward the door. "We can go if you want to be alone."

Brea's laugh electrified the room. "You have icicles on you. I wouldn't send you back out there. You should have some more coffee."

She scooted over, allowing Royce to take a seat next to his wife. Brea patted the spot next to her on the leather couch. Ward shrugged out of his coat and took a seat next to her. The light scent of pine and cold wind still clung to her. Awakened his senses. As did the heat in their locked gazes.

Shana brought out a tray of Danish pastries and small dessert plates, setting them on the coffee table. Chuck shoveled one of the cheese-and-berry Danish pastries onto his plate, and then sat across from Shana at the small table.

Naomi took a sip of coffee before clearing her throat. "Our mom's parents made sure we heard local legends directly from them, not from a book. To keep our heritage alive."

Ward was surprised for a moment. While he recalled reading that the Steele kids had Native Alaskan relatives on their mother's side, he hadn't given it any thought. Hearing this now, from Naomi, showed him more facets of Brea's childhood. "What was your favorite story?"

"'The Legend of the Qalupalik,'" Brea said softly, then glanced at Naomi for her to confirm.

"Yes," Naomi answered. "Qalupalik was green and slimy and lived in the water. She hummed and would draw bad children to the waves. If you wandered away from your parents, she would slip you in a pouch on her back and take you to her watery home to live with her other kids. You would never see your family again. Our grandmother used to tell us that one, and I think it was to get us to behave."

Had Brea thought something like that had happened to her? In a way, it had—except she wasn't bad. No one should endure what she had.

Naomi looked at everyone over the top of her cup. "The story scared us when we were younger, and then once Brea taught us how to be mermaids, we girls embraced the story. We also liked the werewolf legend about the Adlet. They had the lower body of a wolf and the upper body of a human, like a centaur. After Brea was…gone…Broderick and Marshall tried to hunt one once. They had to turn back, though, because I tagged along, and Aiden followed me…"

Ward was only half listening as he registered the warm press of Brea's leg against his own. He could feel her nerves calming as they touched. How was it that he'd developed that ability to read her so clearly? The knowledge knocked him off-balance a bit, though he was only too glad for the excuse to drape his arm around her shoulders.

Shana leaned forward. "What happened?"

Naomi tore off a piece of the pastry. "I took the little twerp home. I was worried about Marshall being so sad and didn't want him to lose out on something fun, so I had to be the grown-up and take Aiden back."

Brea stood, glancing through her thick hair at him. Gave him a wink. An ease rested on her lips. He smiled up at her, enjoying the lightness in the air in this RV. "Can I get refills for anyone?"

No one took her up on the offer.

Brea opened the refrigerator for the creamer since she'd used all the rest set out. Ward's eyes followed her curves. The real, genuine smile that reached her eyes.

She closed the door, then frowned. She stared at a framed photo tucked into a shelf near the refrigerator, her expression frozen, other than furrowing her brow. Then her hand lifted and she touched one picture, her face paling.

Worried, Ward stood and walked the two steps to her, protectiveness surging. "Is something wrong?"

Brea's hand shook and she set the creamer on the counter. "Chuck, I recognize you four Mikkelson kids in this photo. That's you, Glenna, Trystan and Alayna. That's your mom and that must be your father. But who are the other two?"

Chuck rose to join them. "Actually, that's not my mom. That's Trystan's mom—who gave him up to Jeannie to adopt not too long after that." He pointed to the other blonde woman, whose face had been in the shadows. "That's Mom. And this—" he pointed to the other man "—that's Uncle Lyle."

Brea's face paled, and she wavered on her feet.

"He was there at the airport that day, and so was…"
Her finger wavered over the photo, back and forth
between the two women. "One of them."

Eight

Brea felt dizzy, her brain awash with fragmented memories that she couldn't seem to blend into a whole image because of the jagged edges. She recalled seeing the couple at the airport, the man and a woman.

Tension mounted, making her grind her teeth down so hard, her jaw ached. But she couldn't unlock the pressure. Couldn't stop the submerged, underwater sounds in her ears as panic and anxiety took root. All the research she'd done on the Mikkelsons had involved their finances. Their business. She hadn't looked at pictures.

It was the visuals that unlocked the memory.

"Which woman?" Shana asked Brea while resting a comforting hand on Chuck's shoulder.

The spacious luxury RV suddenly seemed to crumple in around her. Air tasted heavy as the hint of knowledge danced in her memory.

Silence wouldn't help her, though. Willing her jaw open and fighting past the panic in her chest, Brea stared at the photo. "I'm pretty sure it's the other one and not your mom, but I can't be certain."

Brea tried to bring the image from the day of the crash into better focus in her mind's eye.

Chuck strode closer to the shelves to look at the photograph, his face somber. "What reason would my uncle and aunt have to harm your family?"

Royce leaned forward, elbows on his knees as he addressed Chuck. "To make your dad's company have less competition so he could make more money?"

Ward put a protective arm around Brea's shoulders. "That's farfetched. What kind of people were they?"

Chuck let out a sigh. He crossed his arms, crumpling his plaid shirt. "We didn't know them well. And when my aunt gave up Trystan for adoption to Mom, our connections with my aunt and uncle faded away."

Shana touched his arm. "Alayna said she thought she overheard something suspicious about your uncle, but was too young to understand. And she thought she saw him at the rodeo a couple of months ago."

Brea sagged to sit. She'd been searching for answers, and now that it seemed she might have them, it overwhelmed her as she realized how much pain could ripple out from this discovery. "Chuck, I'm so sorry. I know this can't be easy for you."

Her heartbeat hammered in her ears. For years she'd thought about this kind of clue. Fantasized about finding a lead to what had caused the event that was the dividing line in her life—the point of turmoil that had sent her spinning for years afterward. Yet in all of her imaginings, this had been a triumphant moment.

In the abstract, the idea of foul play from anyone on the Mikkelsons' side had seemed like an easy answer. But now? Sitting in Chuck's RV, watching his face turn from shock to something like rage and pain…now it was real.

And she wasn't sure of anything.

Not that she had much to stand on in terms of things she was sure of, or solid evidence to pursue. She took a deep breath, catching the aroma of leather, coffee and Ward's aftershave. She anchored herself with Ward's comforting touch.

Chuck cleared his throat. "Whatever the truth is about my mother's family, I want to know the full extent."

"And if that hurts the rest of the family? Your mom? My dad? The business?" She took another breath. "I thought learning the truth would make me happy, but now that I know you all better, it's so much more confusing than it felt when I came back the first time…" Heat rushed to her face, embarrassment over how she'd snuck into their lives with a fake identity. "I'm sorry for the whole Milla Jones deceit."

Shana looked at Brea with concerned eyes and genuine compassion. "I've had amnesia. I understand how difficult it is to put the pieces together when you don't even know who you can trust." She reached to squeeze her hand. "The best thing to do—truly, the only thing to do—is live in the moment."

Could it be that simple? In a life so very complicated, she desperately wanted something that simple. To be able to grasp joy with both hands. With Ward sitting next to her, his aftershave in her every breath and the memory of his touch so tempting in her memory, she found herself grateful for Shana's advice. For her understanding.

Because right now, Brea couldn't imagine recovering from this day anywhere else but in Ward's arms. So she planned to seize the moment and act on her impulse to be with Ward, whatever that meant for the future, as she learned who was responsible for her mother's death.

In the hotel bar two hours later, Ward leaned forward, palms pressing into the rose-quartz bar countertop. He ordered two drinks—a winter ice-cap ale for him and a glass of sparkling rosé wine for Brea. The bartender smiled as he handed the beverages over to him.

Passing the wineglass to Brea, Ward settled back into the leather-backed barstool. The Petru, the most exclusive hotel in town, had been decorated with attention to sophistication. Rustic lights hung, illuminating the pecan-wood shelves and succulents. A live jazz quartet was awash in soft lights on the small stage.

Brea's hair swept upward, a deep side part letting her bangs fall into her face. The proximity of her dark hair seemed to make her blue eyes brighter in this dimmed light. She raised her glass to his beer stein. The clink affirmed the electricity between them in spite of the hellish revelation back at Chuck's RV.

Ward had told her the suite still needed to be cleaned and had suggested they snag drinks at the hotel bar. That had been the first and only lie he had ever uttered to Brea.

Instead the hotel staff was busy finishing the romantic surprise he'd planned for her.

He hoped she would enjoy the gifts he'd ordered. He sensed a shift in her. Something about her body language hinted that she was backing off her no-sex-for-now rule. At least he hoped so. He wanted to tread warily after the emotional afternoon she'd had. Shana had agreed to do more research into Chuck's aunt and uncle, but no one knew where they lived.

There were reasons people hid from their family. And usually those reasons were not good.

Brea grinned. "That RV of Chuck and Shana's was pretty impressive."

Just when he thought he understood her, she found new ways to intrigue him. "I'm surprised."

"By what?"

He reached out to tuck her silken hair behind her right ear. Savored the touch of skin. "That you like that sort of thing."

"It was bigger than most of the places in the community where I lived during my teenage years." Her face took on a faraway look for a moment. No doubt calling ghosts to mind.

The saxophone crooned, spinning Ward into the past. He pictured his father clutching a jazz cassette tape. Driving music, he'd always claimed.

The day hadn't been without memories for Ward either. "My parents had an RV, although it wasn't anything like the one we rode in today."

"What was your favorite trip with them?"

He turned thoughtful, swirling his drink as the bartender passed by with his hands full of limes and oranges.

Leaning closer, Ward reached for her palm and then traced the outline of her fingers. "I think it was when we drove to Denali National Park when I was twelve. We piled into the RV." Ward could picture the deep purple flowers and snow-crested mountaintops. "We didn't take trips where we couldn't camp. My parents wanted to keep vacations cheap and cheerful. Besides—" he took a sip of his beer "—if we hadn't traveled that way, I would never have experienced bears rummaging through our campsite."

"You didn't come from a wealthy background?"

"I did not," he said. "I come from down-to-earth, working-class folks."

People began to swarm the bar. He squeezed her hand, gesturing toward the plush white sofa in the far left of the jazz lounge. She smiled, nodding her agreement. He'd learned that about her. She liked the quiet corners.

He folded his fingers around hers as he picked their way past the tables, where couples spoke in hushed tones. Settling into the sofa, she stroked his hair. For a moment he leaned into her touch. Leaned into this moment with this sexy woman.

"They must be proud of your success."

His good mood faded. "My divorce was a disappointment to them."

"As I understand it, your ex-wife left you." She reached for his hand, linking fingers and squeezing. "Surely your parents realize that."

Taking a swig of beer, he looked down, feeling the storm grow in his chest. "Well, I'm damn sure not going to let down them or a child ever again."

She touched his arm lightly. "You had no control over what happened with Paisley."

"That doesn't make me feel any better." The words were gravel in his throat. "I just don't want her to think I abandoned her, that she can't trust people. I'm sorry you have to worry about who to trust."

She sketched along his jaw with a gentle hand, a determined fire in her eyes. "What's really unfair is that I've lost my mother. I lost the two people

I thought had adopted me. And yes, it sucks that I don't know who's to blame for this chaos. But I also know I'm alive, I'm here and I'm determined to take charge of my future."

"God, you're incredible." He kissed her palm, lingering along the creamy-soft skin and taking pleasure in the pulse speeding in her wrist.

"I'm not." She blushed, but didn't pull her hand away. "Not really. I'm just a survivor."

"In my book, that makes you incredible."

"Let's stop with the depressing talk." Her pupils widened with desire. "I believe the room should be ready now."

He hoped his effort would pay off. He definitely needed to lose himself in the bliss of tangling in the sheets with Brea. To indulge a connection more intense than any he'd ever experienced.

Definitely, the last thing he wanted was to discuss darker subjects. He had his own painful past to contend with, and while he wasn't interested in the future, he refused to let that past steal from what he shared with Brea in the present.

Brea tapped the key card in her hand as she shifted in her heeled boots. Calf muscles tense as she scanned the key across the card reader. Green lights and a ding sounded, indicating the door was unlocked.

Normally, even high-end hotels had a sterile smell to her. But as she crossed the threshold, she felt like she had stepped into a spring meadow. Scents of flowers clung to the air, immediately upgrading her expectations for this swanky hotel. Had they burned candles to make it smell this great?

Turning the corner into the heart of the modern-looking suite, her pulse skipped a beat. Candles weren't the source of the meadow-like scent.

Instead multiple floral arrangements—tulips, roses, lilies—spiked from large vases on the end tables flanking a crisp beige couch with soft gold throw pillows.

On the coffee table, a huge sunflower arrangement waited in welcome. Her favorite flowers. Next to the clear glass vase sat a silver ice bucket with a bottle of champagne and two glasses. Chocolate-covered strawberries drizzled with what looked like caramel sauce were arranged in a heart shape on a silver platter. But the most surprising feature of all?

A gift wrapped in soft pink paper with an elaborate bow on top.

She was thoroughly stunned—and enchanted.

"Happy Valentine's Day," he said, helping her out of her coat.

"But it's not the fourteenth yet." She was touched by his thoughtfulness, at the way he listened to her passing mention of her favorite flower.

"It will be by midnight, and I wanted to make sure your celebration started spot-on the minute."

"I wouldn't have thought you were a romantic."

She walked toward the rose arrangement, breathing deeply of the perfume.

"Well, it's not my forte," he admitted. "But I'm trying. We may not know what the future holds for us, but I'm sure as hell not ready for things to end."

She arched up to kiss him. "Thank you. It's all perfect."

He looped his arms around her waist, drawing her closer. "When we get back to Alaska, what would be your dream date?"

She blinked fast, her shoulders rising. "Honestly, I'm not sure."

His hands rested just over her bottom, caressing lightly, anticipating more. Much more. "Then pick a type of memory you've been eager to replay since you got back but haven't wanted to visit alone—or with your family members."

"That's what you want to do with your romantic date?"

He kissed her neck, just below her ear, a spot where he'd learned a kiss could turn her knees week. But he still had his arms around her. He had no intention of letting go anytime soon.

"We'll be together and that'll help people believe we're really going out—in the interest of cementing my place at the company, of course. Trust me, since we don't want anyone to be suspicious that I'm not a real boyfriend."

"Well, we can't risk that." She laughed softly, the lilt caressing along his senses and stirring a flame deep in his gut. "What do you say we take some of these flowers and sprinkle petals all over the bed?"

His hands roved lower to cup the sweet curves of her bottom. "I think that is a great idea."

She appreciated that he didn't question her turn-around in wanting him back in her bed. Right now, she just wanted to lose herself in sensation. Kissing him. Savoring the hard, muscled wall of his chest against her while their mouths fused, tongues tangling on their way into the bedroom.

As they passed a vase of roses, he plucked out a couple of stems to carry with them, never breaking his connection to her. His hands roaming all over her body made her blood sizzle in her veins. His lips wandered down her neck and back up again, stirring desire to a fever pitch. Once in the bedroom, he tossed the roses onto the comforter. Longing made her impatient, eager. She peeled off her clothes, watching his every move as he did the same until they were standing—naked and wanting—in front of each other.

When he didn't close the distance between them right away, she retrieved one of the roses from the bed and trailed it over her face. Down her neck. Dipping it between her breasts in a seductive move that made his pupils widen with desire.

He picked up the other roses and began plucking the petals off, tossing them onto the comforter until nothing was left but the stems. He tossed them aside and strode toward her, his gaze intent. Heated. He wrapped his arms around her and lowered her to the bed. The scent of him mingled with the perfume of the crushed petals.

Her body was so in tune with his; no words were needed. They met in a blend of taste and touches that set her senses on fire. The crackle of the condom package registered dimly a moment before he nudged apart her thighs. She wrapped her legs around his waist and welcomed him into her body.

Their hips synched up, the rolling of hers in time with his powerful thrusts that sent shimmers of sensation tingling all over. The petals were satin against her back, and Ward's bristly chest a sweet abrasion against her breasts.

She knew from their other lovemaking that they would take their time with the next coupling. For now, it was about a frenzied need charging through both of them.

All too soon her release crashed through her, without warning. There was no staving off the wave of bliss. It consumed her and she let it, wanting the all-encompassing sensation to drown out everything but this powerful connection. His thrusts quickened, and she could feel his muscles tighten in anticipation of his own orgasm as he joined her in completion.

His elbows gave way and he blanketed her body with his, her legs still locked around him. His face buried in her neck, his breath fanned over her shoul-

der. She held tightly to him, unwilling to let go of
this moment.

Because as much as she'd worked to convince
herself this was just a passing fling, that sex with
Ward was a release for all the other emotional turmoil in her life, she couldn't ignore the deepening
bond between them.

A fake relationship turning real.

Which might not be an issue if it hadn't been for
his ties to her family. If she found the answers to her
past that would allow her to fully reunite with the
Steeles, she and Ward would be circulating in close
proximity. When their relationship crashed, there
would be no escaping the painful fallout of him staying in her life.

She would have found the truth, and her family,
only to lose the man she was coming to care about.

Ward fluffed a plush pillow and set it behind
Brea's still-damp hair. The scent of rose petals per-
meated the air. Scattered petals on the floor and on
the bed. From the spa tub, where they'd made love
later. Framing this moment in the kind of romantic
hue he'd hoped to execute but wasn't sure someone
like him could pull off.

He'd carried the small present into the bedroom
with him earlier. Now he pulled it off the nightstand,
knocking the glass of water ever so slightly. He sat
across from her on the bed. They were at ease with
each other in a way that tempted him all the more.

Placing the box into her hands, he smiled. She squinted at him, pulling the ribbon until the bow collapsed. Brea tossed the ribbon at him as she tore the pink wrapping paper. It drifted to the ground in her eagerness.

Her face lit with surprise as she touched the leather-bound journal and pens. "I'm not sure it's a romantic gift. Felicity mentioned you'd been journaling and I thought this would…well…"

She leaned forward to kiss him, briefly but so sweetly. "It's perfect. I'm touched that you went to so much trouble to find something personal." Her fingers skimmed along the gold embossing on the journal cover. "But I don't have anything for you."

"You're not supposed to. Valentine's Day is about the woman." Seeing her happy was gift enough for him.

"You are a charmer, aren't you?" She held the journal and custom-pen set to her chest.

"I wasn't sure you would accept jewelry." If she wanted jewels, he would gladly shower her with them. But something told him those years in the secluded community had given her grassroots kind of values. For that matter, Jack Steele was one of the most down-to-earth billionaires Ward had ever met. Maybe she'd had those kinds of values all her life.

"I may have started out my life in a wealthy family, but I spent my teenage years learning about frugality."

"Living off-the-grid."

"Yes, believe it or not, I can make my own soap," she said with an impish pride.

In his mind's eye, an image of a teenage Brea came to mind. Slaving away at creating lavender-infused soap with a rugged determination.

"I do believe it. You're a resourceful survivor."

She blushed, then looked away with embarrassment under the guise of thumbing through the journal. "What about your childhood?"

"I'm an only child. My parents owned a small business in Fairbanks. They ran a barber shop outside the base that catered to military personnel. They worked hard to put me through college." He stroked her thigh with a gentle touch.

"Are they still living there?"

He chuckled. "They retired to a condo on the beach in Florida."

Leaning over her, he grappled for his phone to show her photographs of his parents' newly renovated Venice Beach condo.

But as he swiped his phone to life, his heart hammered heavily.

A missed call.

From Paisley.

Brea set aside her journal. "Is something wrong? You look worried."

He was. Very.

He thumbed Redial while telling Brea, "It's my stepdaughter. She called—which her mother hasn't let her do before…"

The call went to voice mail. Two more tries later, the same. His worry amplified. The one time his child had reached out to him over this last year, and he'd missed the chance to be there for her.

Nine

The next evening, Brea went through the motions of enjoying Valentine's Day for everyone else's sake. Shana and Chuck had gone to so much effort to throw a dinner party for their visitors at their temporary home in the converted barn.

A long, rough-hewn farmer's table was set with heavy stoneware. Shana declared their meal to be completely composed of foods signature to North Dakota, from the creamy *knoephla* soup to the grilled walleye. They were just finishing the kuchen—rhubarb cake.

It should have been a lovely evening, but the strain of the renewed investigation into the Mikkelson relatives definitely circled around Brea's mind. And

Ward's tension from yesterday's missed call from Paisley still hummed just below the surface, too.

Brea wished she could ease Ward's ache over the loss of his stepdaughter. He'd finally reached his ex-wife, who'd informed him that she and her new husband had gone on a family vacation and Paisley had gotten homesick. Brea heard the woman insist again that she had nothing against Ward, but Paisley had a new "daddy" now. That it would be easier for all if Ward just faded away.

Those words still made Brea's chest go tight. She knew firsthand how much it hurt to have a father fade away inexplicably. But telling Ward as much would serve no purpose.

Luckily, the others at the table hadn't seemed to pick up on that tension during the day, when they'd toured the office buildings, or this evening, at dinner. Shana had proudly shared her husband's gift to her in honor of Valentine's Day—a donation to the foster-care system. In addition to buying her a "stakeout kit" of chocolates. Apparently the two of them sat on stakeouts together when Shana had to follow an investigative lead.

Royce had bought his wife a spa day and a pair of stunning diamond earrings. Naomi beamed as she touched them throughout the meal. This gesture elicited a matching, happy grin from the normally poker-faced Royce.

And as Brea sat listening to everyone, voices drifting up to the high barn ceiling, her mind was filled with a memory of her older brother being dared to hang from the rafters of the boathouse like a bat. She couldn't remember if she'd dared him or if Naomi had. In those days their actions were so tied to each other.

Ward repeated his line that Valentine's Day meant a day of pampering for the women. As such, the men cleared away the stoneware dishes and delicious food.

While they worked, Brea watched her twin pace in the living room of the converted barn. While Chuck and Shana's home was being built, they lived in the rustic beauty that had been reborn as a home. The exposed beams kept the smell of wood heavy in the air. She could hear Naomi coo into the phone, wishing her twins a good-night.

Shana moved down to take a seat next to Brea. She stacked a plate and handed it to Chuck, who'd come back in for the remaining dinner dishes. After sharing a sweet glance with her husband, Shana turned back to Brea. "Brea, you're quiet this evening. In fact, you've been quiet all day. Is something wrong?"

Brea nodded, looking at the remaining wine in her glass. As if all of the answers to her life could be read in the drip patterns. It worked for tea leaves, or so her adoptive parents said.

"I just have a lot to think about. But it's been a lovely working vacation. Thank you."

Shana nodded knowingly. "I'll keep you posted daily on what I learn about Jeannie's brother and sister. I've already got a line on the two of them, up near Fairbanks."

Brea shivered with anxiety. "That's a little too close to home for my peace of mind."

"Stick close to the family." Shana squeezed her hand, but her eyes were also dead serious. Clearly she wasn't taking this lightly, and that meant the world to Brea after feeling so alone. "You'll be well protected."

"Thank you. I'll let you know what I discover, as well." At least Brea hoped she could find the trust to make that leap. She'd been keeping things to herself for so long. "I have to confess, I'm worried about what will happen to the family if it turns out Jeannie knew something about that plane crash all those year ago."

"Would it help if I'm sure she didn't?"

Again, Brea's jaw tightened. Certainty of that kind seemed impossible.

"I wish it could." Brea had no reason to suspect Jeannie. Certainly nothing had turned up on that useless flash drive. Something she still hadn't confessed to Ward. "I've imposed on your Valentine's Day long enough. We should go. Marshall's flying us back tonight, since Naomi and Royce are missing the twins more than they expected."

"That's sweet. They're wonderful parents." Shana's face carried a longing that was impossible to miss. She blinked fast and plastered a smile on her face. "Luckily Marshall has slept the day through, so he's

rested and cleared to fly you back tonight. There's a
bed on the plane if you want to sleep."

"That's wonderful that he can be so flexible,"
Brea said. "I just realized we've kept Marshall from
Tally on their first Valentine's Day."

Marshall hadn't joined them for any of the events,
which was no surprise. He wasn't particularly interested in the family business, and his significant other
was back in Alaska. He spent most of his time on the
family ranch, in the original Steele homestead.

Shana said, "Marshall told me that Tally had a
study session to attend for college. She's begun pur-
suing a degree in social work. He assured me that
they have a day picked out to celebrate and he has
an incredible gift for her. But yes, I see your point."

"She seems to understand he isn't the most romantic man on the planet. But he's a man of character,
of strength. Like our dad."

Ward's familiar boot-falls called Brea's attention,
and she couldn't help but think of how he too was a
man of character and strength. Her breath hitched at
the thought, bringing to mind the possibility that this
was the kind of man a woman could fall for. Ending their affair was going to be more difficult than
she'd imagined.

He moved back into the dining, and she was hit at
once by his magnetism. Ward was a towering, char-
ismatic man who drew her attention by the sheer
force of his eyes.

She could see the strain still lingering on his face

from worry about Paisley. She could only hope she was able to offer him some of the comfort he'd given her the night before. Except she knew it would be more than physical comfort. Every time they were together, every revelation they shared, chipped away at the protective walls she'd built around her heart.

For a woman well versed in hiding, she was finding it impossible to dodge the fact that he was an impossible man to resist on so many levels.

The flight home had been uneventful. Ward was relieved to see Brea gaining confidence with air travel. There were so many places he would like to go with her. His job took him around the world, and having her at his side would be incredible. Images filled his mind of making love to her in Paris, in a room with a view of the Eiffel tower, and in Australia, on an outback excursion.

The possibilities were endless.

For now though, even thinking of being with her in his penthouse apartment stirred him to a near-painful need. Luckily, once the plane landed, she didn't even question him driving them both to his place. Her overnight bag was already packed from their trip, so she had everything she needed.

The private elevator rose with them inside. He'd been given use of the penthouse apartment in the Alaska Oil Barons, Inc., building while he house hunted. The penthouse had previously been inhabited by the Steeles and Mikkelsons, if someone had to work late or weather was particularly treacherous.

The space offered a beautiful view of the mountains. He liked to start his day at the wooden kitchen table with a cup of coffee in a stoneware mug, just looking at the view. But coffee and mountain views were pretty far from his thoughts as the elevator door opened, revealing the space that was more than generous.

Exposed beams made the penthouse feel a bit like a country cottage. Elegant lantern light fixtures hung suspended from the ceiling. Their reflected glow gleamed on the polished wood floors and dark leather furniture. A good place to be. But certainly not a forever home.

Ward had been delaying his own home search, perhaps out of some foolish hope that he'd figure out a way for his stepdaughter to spend time with him. If that happened, he would need to pick a place to accommodate her. If she didn't come? He would just buy a condo much like this. That turmoil over Paisley reminded him all the more of the risk of an emotional connection with Brea, a connection that was growing in spite of his intentions otherwise.

He shoved the painful, futile thought aside and focused on the gorgeous woman beside him. He was in this for sex and yes, to comfort her through this transition back into the family.

But no more than that.

Still, he couldn't take his eyes off her. No one

would have guessed she'd spent the night sleeping on an airplane. Her cable-knit sweater hugged her curves, and something told him the sweater had been hand knitted. Perhaps from her days in the small community? Her sleek black hair was swept back in a high ponytail.

Already his fingers itched to pull her hair free and run his fingers through the silken length.

"Brea…" His voice was hoarse with longing.

She flew into his arms, their kiss one of deep longing, the mating of tongues and need. Was she just seeking comfort?

"Brea," he said again. "Are you sure?"

"There are a million reasons why we shouldn't do this, but all I can think of is the reason we should. I want this, want you, so very much."

He agreed, the same need burning inside him. The feel of her body against his had him throbbing, aching to be inside her. And to hear she wanted him too stoked the fire hotter.

All day, every day, she filled his thoughts. He couldn't get her out of his mind. She was damn near driving him wild. He found himself imagining her naked when he should be focused on work.

He halted the thought because work was the last thing he wanted to think about right now.

Their legs tangled as they walked deeper into the penthouse. He yanked off his coat. Her coat followed, slipping off the sofa to the floor. His hands eagerly touched her side. Helped her out of her sweater. As they passed the control panel on the wall, he flicked the switch to start a blaze in the fireplace, the flames casting golden light.

Three steps later, they were naked and kneeling on a bear rug in front of the hearth. The crackle echoed the need inside of him. He started to angle her down and she stopped him with both hands pressed to his chest. With a siren's smile, she gently pushed him onto his back, the bear rug silky soft underneath him.

And he was more than happy to oblige.

Brea straddled his hips, over him in a beautiful display of creamy flesh. He cradled her breasts in his hands while she released her ponytail, her hair gliding free over the shoulders, along his hands. Raw need pumped through him.

Thankfully he'd snagged a condom from his wallet and had it ready to use. She plucked the packet from his hand and sheathed him with slow…oh so slow…precision. He bit his bottom lip in restraint.

Her hair swinging forward, she eased herself over him, taking him inside her. The sweet clamp of her warmth had him gripping her hips, slowing her to make this last for them.

He wanted to lose himself in her, in the mind-numbing bliss he experienced when she was in his arms. The soft curves of her body filled his every thought, shutting out the rest of the world.

Exactly what he wanted, what he needed—her.

She rolled her hips, meeting his thrusts, her hands flat on his chest, caressing. His fingers glided down from her shoulders. The sweet curves of her breasts filled his hands. He relished the way her nipples pebbled at his touch. Giving her pleasure pleasured him. He wanted to taste every inch of her.

One night, one week or even four wasn't enough to be with her.

The thought blindsided him, stealing his breath. She shouldn't be this important to him this fast.

"Tell me what you want," he whispered in her ear.

"You," she whispered, her voice husky, "I just want you."

The raw need in her tone sent a rush of pleasure through him. He reached between her legs to touch and tease the sweet bundle of nerves.

Kittenish moans rolled up her throat and became cries of release that sent him over the edge with her. Wave after wave of ecstasy washed over him. Brea bowed forward, her chest flush against his. His heart hammered in the aftermath, their sweat-slicked bodies sated.

He lost track of how long they had lain together, the heat of the fireplace keeping them warm as their perspiration cooled. Soon he realized she'd drifted off to sleep. Smiling, he stroked her hair gently. Then he eased her from him and onto the rug. She gave a sleepy sigh of protest.

Quietly, he pulled a throw pillow from the sofa, along with a cashmere blanket to spread over them. He pulled her closer to his side and she rested her head on his chest.

He couldn't deny the truth.

She was becoming important to him emotionally, in a way that surpassed even attraction and that was dangerous for him in ways that had nothing to do with the company. He needed to keep this simple, about the attraction. It couldn't be more. Although he couldn't deny that he wanted them to keep exploring the chemistry.

If he could just figure out how to do that without risking his already battered heart.

Morning sun gleamed through the windows as Brea stretched in bed. But not her bed. She'd slept over at Ward's, sleeping in because they'd arrived home so late and then made love. She reached to find the space beside her empty and cool. The indentation on his pillow tugged at her heart. She leaned forward to breathe in the scent of him.

It was becoming easy to fall into a routine with him, and she didn't want to think about what that meant for when the time came for them to end their relationship.

A shirtless, muscular Ward entered the room with a breakfast tray with two plates of breakfast burritos— made with corn tortillas, fried eggs with avocado slices, cheese and cilantro. Her mouth watered. He'd also brought coffee and juice.

"Ward, you're going to spoil me." The words escaped in a sigh.

He set the tray on the bed and slid in beside her.

"I'm making up for all the travel we had to do on Valentine's Day. I know we're not a real couple, but I feel I owe you more." She felt her smile turn cold at the reality of his words. He seemed to notice the waver of expression, adding, "Damn, and I'm not even sure if that came out right."

"You only spoke the truth. We're not a real couple."

Although it certainly felt real enough to Brea right now as they sat together, naked on the bed, enjoying breakfast.

"We're sleeping together, and I want us to keep on sleeping together." His now-familiar gravelly tone ceased to reassure her.

Brea avoided meeting his eyes by reaching for coffee. "We have a couple of weeks before the board meeting and the vote."

"You could really just hit our deadline and then walk away even after we've shared a bed, calling it over, cold turkey?"

Was that a request for more? And if so, was she even ready for that?

Neither option felt viable. Or made sense. All the same, his request hit her hard. She still didn't know who she was—whether she belonged with the Steeles or if her adoptive family had been right. Whatever that truth was, could she reconcile with her blood relatives?

She wasn't sure what to do.

"That's what we agreed to," she said, sipping her

coffee, not in the mood to savor anything delicious while talking of their uncertain future. She could barely deal with the present.

"And if we decide to change the rules and take things one day at a time?" He looked so hot with the blanket draped over his waist, his broad chest on display.

"Like a real relationship?" Her chest went tight with anxiety as she thought of how their "dating" had started and what she'd done in his office. "You don't even know me, not the real me. I'm the person who's hidden from her family because I was too scared to risk their rejection. I'm not honest—"

"Brea, you went through—"

"Stop. Let me finish." She needed to tell him the truth, because even if she dared to think about something more with him, that couldn't happen without honesty. Even if that revelation cost her any chance at even two more weeks. This was a big chance she was taking, but she didn't have any other option. If people had been honest with her, her life wouldn't be so complicated now. She'd come in search of truth.

Which meant she needed to start dealing in truth, too. She had to hold herself to the same standards she was holding for others. Whatever the cost. "I'm an adult and I know right from wrong. The day you found me in your office, I was stealing files from your computer."

Breath catching in her throat, she waited for his response.

"I already know." His voice dropped an octave.

Shock slashed through her. "You already know? For how long?"

"I suspected when I found you," he explained without even a hint of anger in his voice. "I had my IT guy run a test to check which files you accessed. They're fairly benign. I'm not happy you did it, but it's a nonissue, security wise."

Nothing significant. That lined up with her estimation of the files. She exhaled a hard sigh of relief. Then she realized what his words meant. "Yet you never said anything to me."

"Since there was nothing in that batch of data that could be harmful to the business by betraying trade secrets, I didn't see the need to make an issue of it."

She'd pushed the envelope of honorability too far when she'd pretended to be another person to get a sense of the Steeles without the pressure of a reunion. She deserved for them to be angry with her, and yet they weren't.

She'd pushed the boundaries again by stealing files from Ward. Again she deserved anger, and again that wasn't the reaction she received. Her eyes burned, and she blinked back tears. "But I'm a liar."

He bit into a piece of toast. "And I'm a CEO. We all have our flaws."

"You're letting me off the hook too easily." Guilt piled up inside her. She didn't deserve to be let off the hook.

"Maybe that's because I feel like I know you better now and I'm starting to care for you."

His words hung in the air between, drawing the oxygen from her lungs. She wasn't ready for this kind of talk. Theirs was a fake relationship, a fling. If he pushed the point, what would happen?

Was she scared? Hell, yes. An affair had been risky enough to her heart. But this? And what if he pushed the point? When she'd thought about the cost, she hadn't really considered this could be an all-or-nothing moment.

She stirred a spoon through her coffee to avoid looking into his eyes—or letting him see hers. "Are you sure you're in the right frame of mind to be having this discussion now, given how upset you are about Paisley? Can't we just…be in the moment? Or if you want to be upset, because you have every right to be, then let me comfort you. That's what I would do if something more was really happening between us."

Giving felt more comfortable than taking.

Looking up through her lashes, she blew on her coffee, half hoping he would run if pushed, because considering anything more scared her to her toes.

"There's nothing you can do to help with this," he said tightly, a hint of anger lacing his words.

"Why do you want to continue this relationship, even one day at a time, if we can't discuss the things that are important in our lives?" She held up a hand.

"Or rather, you want me to talk and share, but you're not willing to do the same."

Anger bubbled in his bright blue eyes. They narrowed, and she felt a bitter victory in knowing she was pushing him away and he was taking the bait.

Then his eyes narrowed even further. "Nuh-uh. What's really going on here?"

Panic welled inside her.

"Ward, this is getting too real, too big for me to handle when there's so much unsettled in my life. I can barely remember my own past clearly without people helping me." And she'd been abandoned more times than any one woman should ever have to be... She couldn't take the risk that he seemed to want her to take.

But telling him that part was more vulnerability than she wanted to show. He was already pushing so much faster than she was ready to go.

If only she didn't have to look at the hurt in his eyes. "Brea, we're already in a relationship. Why are we arguing about the label? Call it fake if you want, but I think we both know the feelings are getting pretty damned real." He touched her knee, and heat spiked inside. "The attraction we feel is pretty damned real."

Her shoulders tensed. He was asking for too much. She wasn't ready. "Are you sure it's me you want and not just a replacement family for the one you lost?"

His hand jerked away and his head snapped back as if he'd been slapped. "That's a low blow."

"Not if it's the truth." She wanted him to deny it.

"Sure we started things with some calculated agendas. Have you considered I wasn't just a buffer? That you only want me as an excuse to stay close to your family without actually committing to facing your past?"

Speaking of low blows. His words knocked around inside of her, painful, and maybe even partially true. And if it was even the least bit valid, she'd been horribly unfair to him.

She needed to run, fast. She needed her own space, the quiet of her apartment; she couldn't handle his expectations. Her eyes stung. She was dangerously close to bursting into tears over losing what they'd shared. But she couldn't give him what he wanted, and she did care too much to hurt him, especially after all he'd been through.

Determined to save her pride, if not her heart, she wrapped herself in the blanket to shield herself for a bolt to the bathroom, where she could get dressed.

And hide her tears.

She looked up at him and whispered, "Gargoyle…"

Then she walked out.

Because there was no safe word for the kind of situation she was in now.

Ten

Ward had thought his world had exploded when he'd divorced. He'd also thought he would be insulated from that kind of pain again.

But losing Brea had opened up that old wound all over again.

Ward couldn't deny the truth. He missed Brea, wanted her in his life, but seeing those tears in her eyes made him realize just how high the stakes were. She'd already been hurt too much by people claiming to care for her. Even though he was in this emotionally, he wasn't sure he could manage a forever commitment. He refused to let her be hurt again. So he had to let her go.

Every accidental meeting at the office over the

past two weeks was like alcohol poured on the pain, and he didn't have any idea how to keep from making the same mistakes. He didn't have a clue who to turn to for advice, which told him all the more how badly he'd screwed up his life.

Isolated. Again.

Right in the moment when he'd realized he had started building something with her. Offering her a relationship had been a big move for him.

And now she really wouldn't need him anymore.

He looked down at his notes on his desk. Shana had called, giving reports on the missing aunt and uncle. Police were expecting to pick them up within the week for questioning. They were already wanted in Canada for running a scam on tourists by selling bogus travel packages to tour the North Pole. Now there was a trail connecting them to the plane crash. Crime seemed to cling to their footprints, infiltrating every action.

But as far as Shana could determine, the criminal activity seemed to pertain only to the pair. Bottom line, it didn't appear that Jeannie had anything to do with what her brother and sister had done.

Brea would have a clean slate to reintegrate with her family.

His heart swelled. He was happy for her. Of course. He cared about her a helluva lot. If only there was a way to be sure he wouldn't eventually hurt her if they resumed their affair. If only he wasn't smack-dab in the middle of her family's business.

There was no way to avoid seeing each other if the relationship ended.

Could he handle that? Was he willing to leave the business for her sake?

A knock on his office door drew his attention away from his computer. "Yes?"

The door opened to reveal Felicity Steele, the social worker married to Jack Steele's brother, Conrad. "I'm just dropping off the reports from the meeting."

"The meeting?" His mind reeled as he went through his mental schedule. Realization dawned on him. "Oh, hell, the meeting."

He hit himself on the forehead. How could he have forgotten he was supposed to have met with the Alaska Oil Barons, Inc.'s, charity foundation for the revealing of the new therapy-dog program?

"Please accept my apologies. I have no good excuse for not being there, other than I lost track of time. Name the penance and I'll do it." He pulled out his checkbook.

Felicity stepped inside, a folder tucked under her arm. "While we wouldn't turn down money, we can always use extra volunteers for story hour."

His heart ached at the thoughts of all the stories he'd read to Paisley. All the stories he hadn't been able to read after the divorce. And then something shifted inside of him.

He might not be able to show his stepdaughter how much he loved her, but he could channel that and share it with others. "Send me a calendar of available slots, and I'll be there. No forgetting this time."

"Thank you. The kids will love you." She set the file on his desk. "We also still need someone to dress up as the Easter Bunny for the spring party."

Ward laughed, the sound raspy along his raw throat, and even more raw emotions. "Not a chance." Then he tapped the folder. "What's in here?"

"Handouts from the meeting, photos of the dogs and their handlers."

"You could have emailed those to me." He searched her face for her real agenda.

"I could have. But since I was already so close, I decided to pop by." The look in her brown eyes intensified as she touched the manila folder again. "And quite frankly, I'm worried about Brea."

He sat up straight, concern burning his gut. "Is something wrong with her? Is she hurt?"

Horrible scenarios pumped through his mind. Each one put her in a hospital room. Had she leveraged the information Shana had collected and decided to confront the people responsible for the tragic accident that had ripped her family apart? Sure, she'd been impulsive in the past. But something like that…

Felicity shook her head gently, her counselor training apparent. "Not in the way you mean. She's quiet and in retreat, just like you are."

His heartbeat calmed down, but his mouth grew taut over the intrusiveness of her statement.

"Obviously we broke up." Not that it was anyone's business. And yes, he was in one helluva bad mood.

"Must have been over something horrible."

"What do you mean?" He adjusted his tie. Attempted to put himself together. To gain control of the situation. Of everything.

Including his emotions.

"You've both been through so much in the past and yet you're still standing. So to send you both into such a sad state, I can only surmise something bad happened."

He searched for the right words to explain what had wreaked such devastation in his life.

"We had a fight." It sounded lame, even to his own ears as he vocalized it.

"Hmm…" Felicity mulled silently.

Maybe this wasn't intrusiveness on her part, but caring about Brea. And if so, that meant a lot. Ward wondered if he'd found the person to turn to for help after all. "I know you're not my counselor, and I wouldn't want to take professional advantage…"

She sat down in the leather seat across from him. Smoothing her simple purple dress, she gave him a reassuring, genuine smile. "You would like some advice."

"Yes. Brea thinks I only want her in order to replace the family I lost with her family. I accused her of using me to stay close to her family without facing her past." Words came out of his mouth with the intensity of a waterfall crashing down. "Truth

is, I think maybe she was right about me. Divorce
was hell for me. Losing my wife…but also losing
my stepdaughter."

"Divorce is never easy," she said wisely, "and it's
even tougher when children are involved."

He nodded, his throat too tight to speak.

"Sounds as if you and Brea had quite an argument." She steepled her hands. Raising a knowing
brow, she added in a gentler tone, "It also sounds like
when you're finding a person to love, things like common wants and families are important."

Ward's brows knitted together. He stayed silent
for a moment longer. Processing. "So, you're saying it's okay if we were right in what we accused
each other of?"

"If you love each other, then yes." She held up a
hand. "But I don't need the answer. It's something only
you need to know for yourself." She stood and backed
away from his desk. "And I'll leave you with that since
I need to get back to the hospital. Please feel free to
reach out if you need someone to talk to."

Her generous offer hung in the air after she left.
He sifted through what she'd said and stumbled on
a part he'd missed at first.

She'd said something about loving each other.

Love.

He hadn't even given a thought to that. He'd closed
off his mind to letting that emotion back into his life.
That was the one thing he hadn't offered when he'd
asked Brea to keep their relationship going day by

day. She deserved so much better. And he found that he wanted to give her that. He was determined to do so. He'd learned from the past and wanted to commit fully, no holds barred, to a future. With Brea.

He was beginning to realize it wasn't a matter of "allowing" the feeling. Love climbed walls, breached defenses.

Love had claimed him again.

He'd fallen for Brea, and there was no turning back.

Brea had spent two weeks in a daze, most of which she'd spent in her apartment, with ice cream, trying to figure out what to do with her life now that she had a clear path to reuniting with her family.

Now that she'd alienated a man who would be tied to that family far into the foreseeable future.

Sitting cross-legged on the sofa, she spooned up another taste of Moose Tracks ice cream. The television droned on with another romantic film that just made her feel worse about her life. But she couldn't seem to stop.

Family had called to check up on her and she'd made a slew of excuses as to why she was too busy to take them up on their invitations. Every excuse except the real one. She'd cried herself into dehydration. She'd hit the wall.

This was one blow too many.

The only thing that had stirred any interest in her was Shana's call about finding proof of a phone call between Lyle's cell and the airplane mechanic. Shana had turned it over to the cops.

Finally Brea might have the answers she sought.

A knock on the door pulled her from her self-pity. She placed her ice cream down, muted the television and padded to the door. She peered through the peephole and found the last person she expected...

Her father.

Jack Steele stood on her doorstop with a crockery pot in his hands. And a part of her that remembered her father from long ago realized he had his quietly determined look on his face. He wasn't going anywhere.

She opened the door, leaning against the frame. "Hello, Dad. What brings you here?"

He extended his hands. "Caribou stew. It's been cooking all day and I thought you would like some. We've all been worried you've caught a flu bug."

Her eyes burned with tears and she fought hard to blink them back. "Thank you. That's very thoughtful. Come in."

She waved him through and gestured for him to follow her into the kitchen.

His heavy footfalls thudded along her hall rug. "I'm glad to hear you're all right. No offense but you look like you may have a sinus infection."

She wasn't surprised. Her red eyes and nose probably gave that impression. She'd certainly rather everyone believe that than the truth that she'd hurt one of the most honorable men she'd ever met.

She didn't feel up to admitting she'd been crying nonstop.

"I've just been hibernating for a while, thinking things over." Aspects of the truth were slipping out involuntarily. She blew her nose into a tissue, attempting to recover. "How are you doing with everything?"

"What do you mean?" he asked, setting the red crockery container on the counter.

She dropped down onto one of the barstools. "I heard there's a warrant out for Jeannie's brother and sister's arrest. I know that must be hard for Jeannie."

Shana hadn't seen any signs of involvement from Jeannie, and nothing Brea had found indicated otherwise.

"My heart hurts like hell for Jeannie. Lyle's been picked up. We just heard from the police a little while ago. Her sister hasn't been located yet." He lifted the lid off the pot, stirring. "Her family's brought enough grief to her with the way her sister abandoned Trystan. But Jeannie just says Trystan's better off and that he's her son. That she has what matters…her kids… our marriage."

The scent of the stew wafted in the air, stirring childhood memories. This was a family staple, a recipe handed down from her grandmother to her mom.

Jack stirred slowly. "I never have been able to make this as well as your grandma. Naomi seems to have the knack, but she isn't sharing the secret ingredient with me. But it's not bad. I like to cook it. Makes me remember…"

* * *

    Jack stirred the stew, overwhelmed at having all the kids to himself while Mary slept. Of course, the fact that he'd been up half the night with a colicky Aiden could have something to do with that.

    He had the kids helping him cook, and mostly their feedback had been, "But that's not how Mom does it."

    Broderick was chopping the tomatoes, while Naomi and Brea were cutting bunches of thyme into smaller pieces, carefully. Delaney was reading the directions from the recipe card while Marshall made trips back and forth to the pantry.

    They had this locked and loaded. He hoped.

    "Why can't Mom just make this?" Broderick sighed, huffing in exasperation.

    Naomi rolled her eyes at her teenage brother and mimicked him. "Broderick needs his mommy to cook for him."

    "Your mother has been taking care of baby Aiden. She needs a break," Jack said with a patience he was far from feeling. He wanted a nap. Some said he should have hired a sitter, and they did have one on hand, in addition to his wife's mom for emergencies. But he also wanted time with his kids, and he knew they needed him right now, with a new brother in the house. His mother-in-law was with Mary and the baby. They were a family.

    Him, his wife and their six beautiful children.

    "I don't see why that means she can't make the stew. Hers is the best," Brea said, smelling the thyme.

Jack smiled. "It is. But I think we all make a good team. And you know how your mother is always surprising you with things?"

Brea and Naomi exchanged grins, thinking back to their mother's most recent surprise: a playroom she had painted to mimic the Alaskan wilderness when it was too cold to go outside.

"Mmm-hmm." Broderick nodded.

"Well, it would be cool to give your mother a surprise, too."

He loved his wife and kids more than air. He would do anything for them...

The memory curled through Brea as surely as the aroma from the stew. Except this was steaming through from her brain to her heart.

Her father was Jack Steele. And she wanted her family back.

"It was hell for me when I realized you'd been home as Milla Jones and didn't trust us enough to let us know you were alive. I thought I'd lost you all over again. That you didn't care about me."

His words brought those painful months back in startling clarity.

Pain swelled in her chest. A tightness needing release, needing air and light instead of isolated darkness.

"I want you to know, Dad, I was sick for a long time after the crash—very sick. It wasn't like I climbed on that plane one morning and the next morning just decided my family didn't want me." Her inward gaze sorted through those initial months. The bevy of tears that would not stop. "The confusion was more of a gradual thing. I was grieving and alone, and very weak."

He listened with somber eyes. "I'm glad the Joneses kept you safe."

"How can you feel that way about them after they took me from you? Surely they had to know who I was…" A memory filled her head, of those early days after she recovered, of her sitting crumpled on the couch. Clutching her knees to her chest, her voice hoarse from crying and declaring her identity to her adoptive parents. "I told them who I was."

Jack looked down into the soup for a long moment, and she thought she saw his jaw flex for a moment before he looked at her again, with his face returned to calm. "The officer who called us about Lyle… He said the man apparently confessed to a couple of things… He was there at the crash site. He's the one who found you alive. Apparently he wasn't as adept at killing face-to-face as he was at making it happen by proxy. He knew the Jones couple and paid them to keep you until he could figure out what to do. I think they must have decided to protect you from our family because they perceived us as a threat to you."

Her lips trembled. Emotions rolled through her in a chain reaction—relief, grief, rage, all tangling together and making it tough to draw in air.

She gripped the counter for a moment, biting her

lip to hold back a cry that would only upset her father when he'd been through enough. Finally she was able to draw a steady breath. "That's bighearted of you."

"Did they love you?" Jack Steele looked up from the stew again. His steady gaze resting on her.

At first Brea ground down her teeth. Thought back to her life with her adoptive parents. The way her adoptive mother would put a cool cloth on her head when she was sick, or would read the same books she did so they could discuss them. The way her adoptive father would take her with him to work on wiring projects to provide electricity to their small community. "They treated me as if they did."

Jack nodded. "Then I think we have to let it rest with the courts alone if we want a clean slate to reunite as a family."

She knew that couldn't have been easy for her father to say. Because he had just as much—if not more—cause than her to be furious over what had happened, to want vengeance.

She reached out to hug him. "Daddy…"

He hauled her in for a bear hug that was so familiar, she couldn't imagine how she'd ever forgotten it.

"Brea, do you want to tell me what's really been wrong these past two weeks? Because I'm a father of daughters. I recognize the red-eyes-and-ice-cream combo."

He tilted his head toward the open Moose Tracks container on the coffee table in her living room.

With a watery sniffle, she angled back, swiping at her eyes. "I've made a mess of things with Ward."

The past two weeks had been so lonely without him. She'd missed the scent of him, the way he started the day off with a smile, by having a simple breakfast together, how he discussed business with her and genuinely valued her opinion. And right now she wished she could share this news with him.

"You and he are really a couple?" her father asked in undisguised shock. "I thought you two were working some mutually beneficial deal."

"You knew?" she gasped.

He winked. "I'm a damn good businessman."

"Well, it started out as something, um, logical, then became more. And now I've pushed him away."

"Then go get him," her father said simply. "Understand, I love Jeannie every bit as much as I loved your mom. But while your mother was alive, nothing would have kept me from her if I thought there was a chance to reconcile."

And hearing the determination in his voice, she realized, fully, that he really had thought she was dead, along with her mother.

She hadn't been abandoned, or merely forgotten after a short search.

She was loved.

She was a Steele.

And as long as there was hope, a Steele didn't give up.

* * *

Ward cracked his knuckles. A habit he'd picked up when he'd been a teenager. For the most part, he'd been able to kick it. But in moments of stress—before a big meeting or closing a deal—the habit resurfaced.

Of all the times he cracked his knuckles as an adult, none seemed as intense as this time.

He had a lot to lose.

Everything to lose, in fact.

But the lights were on him and he had to tamp down the habit. Play the part of CEO. And if he was lucky, a more important victory awaited him.

As he continued his speech, his mind was hoping he could pull off the win of a lifetime with Brea. No company stockholders' meeting could ever be as important as winning Brea back. He was nearing the end of his speech, which would close out the meeting, and he was coming to the most important part of his presentation.

The general Board of Directors meeting was going as well as he had anticipated. As well as he had hoped for, really. Pleased stockholders in expensive business suits nodded along at Ward's figures and charts.

The meeting was being held on the top floor of the Steele building. It was set up as a dinner gathering, and the clink of silverware on plates around the boardroom table was subtle as he moved through his presentation. He shifted his weight from foot to foot, restless. A trickle of sweat gathered at the nape of his neck. Luckily his collar and suit jacket hid his unease.

Looking out on the audience around the fully set dinner table, his gaze landed on Brea. Ward's gaze took in every alluring detail of her, down to the way her silky black dress and cashmere sweater-jacket accented her curves in simple elegance. Even in the dimmed lighting of the boardroom, he couldn't help but notice her beauty.

But his feelings for her were about so much more than that. The depth of emotion, of love, he felt for her floored him.

She caught him staring as she chewed her steak delicately. The Alaska Oil Barons, Inc., held the philosophy that business was made sweeter by food. A philosophy he agreed with. Breaking bread together had a way of putting people at ease. He quickly searched her face, trying to determine if the food had indeed eased something in Brea.

He didn't want to, but he tore his gaze from hers to look at the stockholders as he finished his speech. The meeting would be over, and his time to win Brea would begin.

He clicked through the slides to a blank screen. "That concludes the business part of my presentation. I want to share some words that are more personal. I feel that's important since we'll all be working together for a long time to come." He grinned. "At least I hope we will."

His remark brought the expected chuckle that helped him transition to the more personal note. "I have had the honor of spending time with Breanna Steele. Some of you may have heard we've been seeing each other. As I've come to know her these past weeks, I've discovered she's an incredible woman of strength and brilliance. Like all the Steeles—and Mikkelsons. I have big shoes to fill around this place, and I look forward to the challenge.

"Should you trust me?" he continued. "I've learned that trust is a cagey thing. It comes with time." He held Brea's gaze. She didn't look away. Instead that electricity danced between them. For a moment he could pretend they were the only people in the room. "And I'm willing to put in the time, the hours, weeks—years, if need be—to make sure I'm your top choice, worthy of the faith you've put in me."

He took a breath before continuing, "Luckily I've got some top-notch role models around here in Jack and Jeannie." He grinned. "And I'm not just saying that to suck up. They're an admirable couple who've welcomed me into the Alaska Oil Barons, Inc., family."

With luck, he prayed they would welcome him into their real family, as well.

He smiled as he stepped off the podium. Board members and shareholders alike clapped. Some clapped him on his back as he walked by. Others shook his hand, offering praise. With the confident gait he was known for, he strode right toward Brea.

He leaned in and whispered into her ear, "Gar- goyle."

She looked at him with wide eyes, before smiling. "You want to leave? Now? This is your party. Your welcome to the company. This is your everything."

She looked around the table at the chatter. To- ward her father, who raised a glass of whiskey in their direction.

"*You* are my everything," he said. "Now let's find somewhere private to talk."

She nodded, discarding her cloth napkin onto her chair. She took his hand, squeezing lightly, her eyes shiny with emotion and even a hint of tears. Her hand shook in his but she didn't let go. A good sign as he led her toward the elevator to his penthouse apartment.

The ride up was silent but filled with fire and magic. Just as it had been the first day they'd met. He led her across the wood floors to the bearskin rug by the already crackling fire.

He planned to pull out all the stops for this, need- ing every ounce of charm to prove to her he was ready to risk his heart again, ready to be a part of a family again, not as a replacement, but as what came next, as where he belonged.

He loved Brea. Truly. Deeply.

They knelt together by the fire. Brea's knee-length

black dress showing her shapely calves. After a moment she tilted her head, curls framing her beautiful face. "Was it my imagination or were you sending me some incredible messages through your speech, in your eyes?"

Clasping her hands, he rubbed his thumbs along the insides of her wrists. "These past two weeks thinking I'd lost you have been hell."

She bit her lip. Swallowing. He saw the pain reflect in her eyes. "For me, too."

"You've worked your way into my heart."

She stared at him, speechless.

"Why are you so surprised? I can't imagine I've hidden how much you mean to me."

"I know we have chemistry..."

He shook his head. Held her hands tighter, inching closer to her. "It's much more than that for me. Brea, I'm in love with you."

Her mouth opened in an O-shape of surprise. Then her eyes welled with tears. "I'm so very glad to hear that. You mesmerized me the first time I saw you, and truly every time after that, with your brains as much as your body. Ward, I'm head over heels in love with you, too."

He spiked his fingers through her hair and guided her head closer for a kiss, one that sealed this moment, this first time they expressed their love for each other.

"I'm so glad you broke into my office."

She laughed lightly before her face turned serious again. She clasped both of his hands, squeezing. "I shouldn't have said those hurtful things to you. I understand how painful it was for you to lose your daughter. It was wrong of me to use that against you in an argument."

Ward swallowed. Needing to make sure Brea knew it was her that he wanted. Not her family. Not anyone else.

She, by herself, was valuable to him. He'd been hurt before, but she was worth taking the risk again.

"Do you really believe I'm using you and your family as a substitute for what I've lost with my stepdaughter?"

She shook her head. The tears still welling in her eyes. "I see now that you're drawn to me—and to them—because this is the kind of family life you want. And that's not a bad thing. I also understand it must be scary for you to risk being a part of that again."

"It's tough…very tough." His chest tightened. But looking into Brea's eyes, he knew this was right.

"It's not easy for men to admit to being afraid."

"True enough." He gave her a wry smile and then stroked her face gently. "I'm sorry for what I said about you using me. There's no way I—or anyone— can fathom all that you've been through."

"I do want my family back. But I also want you. Those two 'wants' are not tied to each other."

"I'm glad to hear it." So damn glad to have this

second chance with her, he kissed her deeply, their breath mingling, their tongues mating.

Brea whispered against his mouth. "I've been thinking about my future."

"Oh, really. I'd like to hear." He kissed her neck softly, launching tingles throughout her.

She ran her hands through his hair. "Royce and I talked in North Dakota about his research and my experiences living off-the-grid. We would like to explore ways we can make resources more accessible to those in far-flung regions."

"That sounds like a great idea, professionally and personally." Ward rested his forehead against hers, breathing in the floral scent of her shampoo. Looking forward to being a part of her life for the rest of their days.

"We have forever together," she said, as if reading his thoughts. "I don't want to keep you from your board meeting."

"I've met my obligations to them. Your family—"

"Our family," she corrected him.

"You truly are an amazing woman. I hope you know that."

"You can feel free to tell me anytime you like." She looped her arms around his neck.

He angled her back onto the bearskin rug, already looking forward to making love to her thoroughly throughout the night. "I hope that means you intend to keep me around."

Her smile lit her eyes and his heart. "I can't think of anything I'd like more than for our relationship to be real. Maybe I'll even break into your office every day."

Epilogue

Two years later

Brea stirred the steaming pot in her kitchen, the scent of caribou stew taking her back to her childhood, in her grandmother's kitchen, with a clear, happy memory.

No panic. No fog. Just a joyful, simple connection to a happy part of her past that she held tight.

The scents of bay leaf and garlic drifted in the light-filled kitchen of her own design, the skylight perfectly positioned to let her look up and see the stars as often as she wanted. It had been Ward's idea when they had built the house just outside of Anchorage. This spot under the skylight was her place to breathe deep and take strength from the natural world, even as she was surrounded by the deep love of her big family.

The Steeles.

The Mikkelsons.

And Ward.

Brea met his gaze across the island as he entered the kitchen. He passed off Broderick and Glenna's daughter, Fleur, to Alayna Mikkelson, who was home from college for winter break. The whole family had gathered in Brea and Ward's home for a combination housewarming party and a viewing of the new episode of *Alaska Uncharted*, featuring Alaska Oil Barons, Inc.

Their family.

"That smells amazing." Ward stepped behind her while she put the cover on the stew.

"I have been tasting as I go, and I can promise you, it will be delicious." She leaned into him while his arms wrapped around her, his hands resting on her stomach.

"How are you feeling?" He kissed a spot beneath her ear, sending a thrill through her even now that they'd been married for a year. "I can take over and you can put your feet up."

"I'm feeling fantastic. And I can't wait for dinner. I've been craving this dish all week."

He nuzzled her neck. "The twins must be hungry."

This week's appointment with the obstetrician had shown a surprise—two babies. They hadn't even told the family she was pregnant yet, so the news would be another cause for celebration tonight. They'd had fun planning their big reveal, finally deciding on a cake for dessert that had a gold topper with two porcelain infants.

"It's a good thing we're telling the family tonight. I can't wait to quiz Naomi about everything twin related that happened with her pregnancy."

She had recovered her own twin bond with her sister, a bond that would only strengthen as they raised their own twins.

Brea was three months along. They'd waited until now to tell because they'd wanted to include Paisley in the celebration. With help from Felicity on how best to approach his ex-wife, Paisley's mother had finally consented for Ward and Brea to have contact, from phone conversations to an occasional vacation. Paisley was here now for her school's winter break, and Brea guessed she was having fun with all of her cousins.

The last time Brea had looked into the great room, she'd seen Paisley in a corner, reading books, side by side with Conrad and Felicity's daughter, Kylie, a teen they'd adopted last year. Seeing the two of them that way—happily reading while warm family chaos unfolded all around them—reminded Brea so much of Marshall.

Another joyful memory.

"Naomi is going to be thrilled. But so is everyone else," Ward assured her as he drew her toward the family room, where the *Alaska Uncharted* episode was playing in the background.

Jack and Jeannie held hands on the couch while Naomi's girls entertained them with the new moves they'd learned in their baby-ballet class. Marshall and Tally came in the back door, stomping snow off their boots from a horseback ride with Conrad and Felicity.

"Did we miss it?" Tally rushed into the living room. "I told them to hurry."

Tally was on winter break too, her college program in social work almost finished. She and Marshall were waiting to have children until she had her degree. The semester before, Tally, Aiden and Alayna had all ended up in the same online history class—a popular local offering since the professor was an expert on native Alaskan tribes.

Apparently Alayna and Aiden's short-lived romance had ended without drama. Aiden seemed happy working in the oil fields while he took classes online, and Alayna was dating one of the company's interns.

Glenna was seated at the desk in the far corner of the room with her toddler son, watching the screen, where Shana's and Chuck's faces were visible. Their three children, siblings ranging from ages two to six, adopted at the same time, took turns pressing their noses close to the camera, waving excitedly as they caught sight of their cousins.

Their blended family kept on blending and adding, but that seemed just right when they had so much love to give.

All was right in Brea's world.

She exchanged looks with Ward, the man who had helped her find her family again, while keeping her sense of self. She liked to think she'd helped him find his family, too. He held her hand in his, his thumb stroking over her knuckles.

"Happy?" she asked him while they surveyed the room of people coming and going.

Before he could reply, Tally hurried over to draw Brea deeper into the room.

"This is your part, Brea. Come see."

Brea let herself be pulled closer to the family even though she and Ward had already seen the *Alaska Uncharted* episode in a preview screening.

Thomas Branch's distinctive voice was narrating about the new Alaska Oil Barons, Inc., Energy Outreach initiative, the effort to bring energy innovations to off-the-grid communities. Brea worked on it with Royce and Delaney, but the online network for dispensing the information had been her brainchild. A path to connect her both lines of her past in a positive way. An overture toward the kinds of communities that helped nurture her when she'd been broken. They were still a part of her.

"I'm so proud of you," Ward whispered in her ear, reeling her closer to rub her shoulders.

His touch warmed her all over and she felt the tingle of tears behind her eyes. The good kind, though.

She'd fought so long and hard simply to find peace, that to discover this well of deep-seated happiness was an incredible bonus.

On the huge flat-screen television, an image of Alaska General Hospital appeared as the host continued his narration. "The Steeles and Mikkelsons have made quite a name for themselves with their charity innovations, as well. The Steele wing of the Alaska General Hospital now has a new children's library, as well as a therapy dog program to comfort the patients."

Isabeau Mikkelson appeared on the screen as the hospital's PR director, commenting on the library that Conrad had personally overseen and the therapy-dog program that Felicity had put in place with Tally's help.

"The pipeline in North Dakota is fully functional now, increasing the reach of the Alaska Oil Barons, Inc. Chuck Mikkelson carries on his father's legacy with the help of scientist Royce Miller, with input from Delaney Steele Montoya and Breanna Steele Benally."

The last bit was drowned out underneath the shouts of "Daddy!" from Chuck's kids as they heard their father's name mentioned. Brea was so happy for him and Shana, forging their own strong family with the love that had inspired her so much two years ago.

"The day-care addition to the corporate offices is state of the art—and put to use by much of the family. And the public has taken note of their trust

in the company when they could have afforded full-time nannies."

The video image panned around the Alaska Oil Barons, Inc., day-care facility, where plenty of the children in this room spent time on a regular basis. While Naomi's girls and Fleur squealed to see themselves on the screen, Isabeau's son and Fleur's brother were both unimpressed, pushing their wooden trains in circles around the girls' feet.

"The stew smells so good!" Tally burst out as the television show came to an end. "I can't wait for dinner, Brea. Can I help?"

Not waiting for an answer, Tally was already halfway into the kitchen, a place she and Felicity had spent plenty of evenings over the last year, since Tally and Marshall lived close by.

Ward kissed Brea's cheek. "I hope that cake is well hidden," he whispered. "Or the cat's out of the bag."

"Ward Bennally, I think I know how to keep a secret. Don't you?" She turned in his arms, surrounded by his strength.

Their love.

Their family.

"Just not from me." He tipped his forehead to hers. "I get to share all your secrets from now on, Mrs. Bennally."

"You already do." She loved this man with a fierceness she couldn't describe. Having him by her side made her feel safe. Whole. And incredibly happy. "I love you, Ward."

"I love you too, Brea." He cradled her face in his hands and stroked his thumbs down her cheeks before he let her go.

Her heart melted a little at his touch. Even two years after she'd fallen in love with him, she knew they had the kind of love that was never going to fade. It was too hard-won. Too precious to them both.

Hand in hand, they joined their family for the real celebration that was only just beginning.

* * * * *

COMING NEXT MONTH FROM

HARLEQUIN®
Desire

Available March 5, 2019

#2647 HOT TEXAS NIGHTS
Texas Cattleman's Club: Houston
by Janice Maynard

Ethan was Aria's protector—until he backed away from being more than friends.
Now her family is pressuring her into a marriage she doesn't want. Will a fake
engagement with Ethan save the day? Only if he can keep his heart out of the
bargain...

#2648 BOSS
by Katy Evans

I have a new boss—and he's hot but irresponsible, a youngest son. If he thinks
he can march into this office and act like he owns the place, he needs to think
again... If only I didn't want him as much as I hate him...

#2649 BILLIONAIRE COUNTRY
Billionaires and Babies • by Silver James

Pregnant and running from her almost in-laws, Zoe Parker is *done* with men,
even ones as sinfully sexy as billionaire music producer Tucker Tate! But Tucker
can't seem to let this damsel go—is it her talent he wants, or something more?

#2650 NASHVILLE SECRETS
Sons of Country • by Sheri WhiteFeather

For her sister, Mary agrees to seduce and destroy lawyer Brandon Talbot. He is,
after all, the son of the country music star who ruined their mother. But the more
she gets to know him, the more she wants him...and the more she doesn't know
who to believe...

#2651 SIN CITY VOWS
Sin City Secrets • by Zuri Day

Lauren Hart is trying to *escape* trouble, not start *more*. But her boss's son,
Christian Breedlove, is beyond sexy and totally off-limits. Or is he? Something's
simmering between them, and the lines between work and play are about to
blur...

#2652 SON OF SCANDAL
Savannah Sisters • by Dani Wade

At work, Ivy Harden is the perfect assistant for CEO Paxton McLemore. No one
knows that she belongs to the family that has feuded with his for generations...
until one forbidden night with her boss means *everything* will be revealed!

**YOU CAN FIND MORE INFORMATION ON UPCOMING HARLEQUIN® TITLES,
FREE EXCERPTS AND MORE AT WWW.HARLEQUIN.COM.**

HDCNM0219

Get 4 FREE REWARDS!

We'll send you 2 FREE Books plus 2 FREE Mystery Gifts.

Harlequin® Desire books feature heroes who have it all: wealth, status, incredible good looks... everything but the right woman.

FREE Value Over $20

YES! Please send me 2 FREE Harlequin® Desire novels and my 2 FREE gifts (gifts are worth about $10 retail). After receiving them, if I don't wish to receive any more books, I can return the shipping statement marked "cancel." If I don't cancel, I will receive 6 brand-new novels every month and be billed just $4.55 per book in the U.S. or $5.24 per book in Canada. That's a savings of at least 13% off the cover price! It's quite a bargain! Shipping and handling is just 50¢ per book in the U.S. and 75¢ per book in Canada.* I understand that accepting the 2 free books and gifts places me under no obligation to buy anything. I can always return a shipment and cancel at any time. The free books and gifts are mine to keep no matter what I decide.

225/326 HDN GMYU

Name (please print)

Address   Apt. #

City   State/Province   Zip/Postal Code

> Mail to the **Reader Service:**
> **IN U.S.A.:** P.O. Box 1341, Buffalo, NY 14240-8531
> **IN CANADA:** P.O. Box 603, Fort Erie, Ontario L2A 5X3

Want to try 2 free books from another series? Call 1-800-873-8635 or visit www.ReaderService.com.

---

*Terms and prices subject to change without notice. Prices do not include sales taxes, which will be charged (if applicable) based on your state or country of residence. Canadian residents will be charged applicable taxes. Offer not valid in Quebec. This offer is limited to one order per household. Books received may not be as shown. Not valid for current subscribers to Harlequin Desire books. All orders subject to approval. Credit or debit balances in a customer's account(s) may be offset by any other outstanding balance owed by or to the customer. Please allow 4 to 6 weeks for delivery. Offer available while quantities last.

Your Privacy—The Reader Service is committed to protecting your privacy. Our Privacy Policy is available online at www.ReaderService.com or upon request from the Reader Service. We make a portion of our mailing list available to reputable third parties that offer products we believe may interest you. If you prefer that we not exchange your name with third parties, or if you wish to clarify or modify your communication preferences, please visit us at www.ReaderService.com/consumerschoice or write to us at Reader Service Preference Service, P.O. Box 9062, Buffalo, NY 14240-9062. Include your complete name and address.

HD19R

*I have a new boss—and he's hot but irresponsible, a
youngest son. If he thinks he can march into this office
and act like he owns the place, he needs to think again...
If only I didn't want him as much as I hate him...*

Read on for a sneak peek of
Boss
by New York Times *bestselling author Katy Evans!*

My motto as a woman has always been simple: own
every room you enter. This morning, when I walk into
the offices of Cupid's Arrow, coffee in one hand and
portfolio in the other, the click of my scarlet heels on
the linoleum floor is sure to turn more than a few sleepy
heads. My employees look up from their desks with
nervous smiles. They know that on days like this I'm
raring to go.

Though it sounds bigheaded, I know my ideas are
always the best. There's a reason Cupid's Arrow swept
me up at age twenty. There's a reason I'm the head of
the department. I carry the design team entirely on my
own back, and I deserve recognition for it.

The office doors swing open to reveal Alastair
Walker—the CEO, and the one person I answer to
around here.

"How's the morning slug going, my dear Alexandra?" he asks in that British accent he hasn't quite been able to shake off, even after living in Chicago for a decade. He's adjusting his sharp suit as he saunters into the room. For his age, he's a particularly handsome man, his gray hair and the soft creases of his face doing little to steal the limelight from his tanned skin and toned body.

At the sight of him, my coworkers quickly ease back.

"The slug is moving sluggishly, you might say," I admit, smiling in greeting.

When Alastair walks in, everyone in the room stands up straighter. I'm glad my team knows how to behave themselves when the boss of the boss is around. But my own smile falters when I notice the tall, dark-haired man falling into step beside Alastair.

A young man.

A very hot man.

He's in a crisp charcoal suit, haphazardly knotted red tie and gorgeous designer shoes, with recklessly disheveled hair and scruff along his jaw.

Our gazes meet. My mouth dries up.

And it's like the whole room shifts on its axis.

I head to my private office in the back and exhale, wondering why that sexy, coddled playboy is pushing buttons I was never really aware of before. Until now.

Don't miss what happens when Kit becomes the boss!
Boss
by Katy Evans.

Available March 2019 wherever
Harlequin® Desire books and ebooks are sold.

www.Harlequin.com

Love Harlequin romance?

DISCOVER.

Be the first to find out about promotions, news and exclusive content!

Facebook.com/HarlequinBooks

Twitter.com/HarlequinBooks

Instagram.com/HarlequinBooks

Pinterest.com/HarlequinBooks

ReaderService.com

EXPLORE.

Sign up for the Harlequin e-newsletter and download a free book from any series at **TryHarlequin.com.**

CONNECT.

Join our Harlequin community to share your thoughts and connect with other romance readers!
Facebook.com/groups/HarlequinConnection

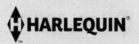

HARLEQUIN®

ROMANCE WHEN YOU NEED IT

HSOCIAL2018

THE WORLD IS BETTER WITH

Romance

Harlequin has everything from contemporary, passionate and heartwarming to suspenseful and inspirational stories.

Whatever your mood, we have a romance just for you!

Connect with us to find your next great read, special offers and more.

Earn points on your purchase of new Harlequin books from participating retailers.

Turn your points into **FREE BOOKS** of your choice!

Join for FREE today at
www.HarlequinMyRewards.com.

Harlequin My Rewards is a free program (no fees) without any commitments or obligations.

MYR18